WOLF M

The sequel to *Oc*

Rachel Stone has been smitten by the curse of the werewolf. From that moment drama and danger have entered her life. As a wolf she stalks the countryside at the full moon. She decides she must return to Ireland from her home in California and contact Madoc, the last of the werewolf clan, and try to get rid of the curse. But can she be cured of this terrible curse? Or is it for life ...?

An exciting series from
THE O'BRIEN PRESS

October Moon has been widely praised and has sold
in many countries and translated into several languages.

'a really good tale of terror' SUNDAY TRIBUNE

'an excellent read ... ten out of ten' AERTEL RTE

Michael Scott

Born and brought up in Dublin, Michael Scott worked in a variety of bookshops, and was an antiquarian bookseller before turning to writing fulltime. First published in 1981, he has written approximately fifty books to date. Married, with two children, he lives in Dublin. His books for young readers include stories from Celtic mythology, fairytales and fantasy, stories of horror and the supernatural.

The *Irish Guide to Children's Books* praised Michael Scott for his 'unparalleled contribution to children's literature'.

WOLF MOON

Michael Scott

THE O'BRIEN PRESS
DUBLIN

First published 1995 by The O'Brien Press Ltd.,
20 Victoria Road, Rathgar, Dublin 6, Ireland.

BRITISH LIBRARY CATALOGUING-IN-PUBLICATION DATA
Scott, Michael
Wolf Moon. – (Other World Series)
I. Title II. Series
823.914 [J]

ISBN 0-86278-420-4

The O'Brien Press receives assistance from
The Arts Council / An Chomhairle Ealaíon.

1   2   3   4   5   6   7   8   9   10
95 96 97 98 99 00 01 02 03 04

Cover illustration: Peter Haigh
Cover design: O'Brien Press Ltd.
Cover separations: Lithoset Ltd., Dublin
Printing: Cox & Wyman Ltd., Reading

This is the curse of the Clan of Natalis:
to take the form of a wolf at the full of the moon...

FROM THE DIARY OF PIERS DE COURTNEY

I am Derg Corra, Fionn Mac Cumhaill's gilly.
I am the Shapechanger.

FROM THE LEGENDS OF FIONN MAC CUMHAILL

DEDICATION
To Courtney and Piers

1

THE FULL MOON WASHED THE BEACH in black and grey, painting the gently lapping waves with a cold silver light.

The creature lay half-hidden in the sand dunes, breathing deeply, heart thumping solidly. Waiting. Its sensitive hearing could detect the vibrations of human voices, the metallic snap and crackle of a radio turned up too high, the roar of their bonfire, the hiss of the surf sweeping in across the beach.

And it could smell them. Above the scents of sea and salt and warm sand, it could smell the odours of the humankind: stale sweat, cheap beer, the stink of gasoline fumes and greasy food burning on a barbecue.

Meat.

Warm meat. Hot and salt.

The creature raised its head, nostrils flaring, heart beating faster, warm saliva flooding its mouth. Then it came to its feet, lips peeling back from savage incisors. A thick curl of saliva dribbled onto the sand and the creature's stomach rumbled. A low involuntary growl came from its throat.

It hungered.

The creature wanted to run, to crash through the crude bonfire, scattering the people. It wanted – needed – the thrill of the chase, to listen to their screams echoing flatly along the beach, it wanted ...

It wanted to hunt.

To hunt and kill and eat.

No

The creature shuddered as if it had been struck.

No.

The beast shook itself and the voice vanished to a whisper. But it was there, always there, troubling, insistent, a human voice, a female voice.

The creature was female, it knew that much about itself. It knew also that it was strong and savage and powerful.

Again, the creature shook herself. The voice was unimportant. It was nothing. What was important now was the chase, the hunt, the fight.

The beast stretched, and walked slowly away from the dunes, gauging the wind and available light, wondering how close it could get to the people before it was spotted. It kept low, scurrying along the sand, belly close to the ground. Fifty paces from the small group it stopped, sinking into the shadows, becoming invisible ... except for its eyes which danced with the reflections of the flames.

There were eight of them, all young adult males, strong and healthy. They each wore identical patterned bands on their arms. Tattoo. The word came unbidden. A clan, the creature realised. Crouching low, it tested the air, smelling a sharp acrid odour. Alcohol. Three of the humans were in a strange, weakened state. Their minds were vague, their senses dulled: they would be no challenge. But the others ... There was one in particular. He was very big for a human and he was a lot

8

older than the others, grey hair tied back in a long pony-tail, long grey beard. He was clearly the clan leader. A fine target.

The beast's moist nose twitched, smelling the foul stink of the clan's two-wheeled metal beasts. Creatures that roar and whose single eye could blaze with blinding light. The humans would attempt to flee on their metal steeds.

No ... no ... no ...

When the clan leader picked up a short glass tube – alcohol – raised it to his lips and began to drink, the beast pounced, snarling viciously.

The leader sputtered and choked, but the beast ignored him. Leaping high, it landed on the back of the nearest man. He screamed, and collapsed to the sand, his arms and legs scrabbling madly. Razor-sharp teeth clicked close to his ear, silencing him.

The creature padded off the man's back and turned to face the others. Most had fled for their wheeled beasts, engines already beginning to roar, but the creature let them go, and faced the leader, who was still seated in front of the bonfire, staring open-mouthed in shock.

He made a grab for something at his side, but even though he was fast for a human, he was far too slow. The creature's teeth closed on his arm – not deeply, but enough to make him drop the long-bladed knife.

The man stood up slowly, keeping his eyes fixed on the terrifying creature, and backed away.

The beast followed him.

The human took another step back. He shouted for help, his voice high-pitched and frightened. There was no reply. He stepped back farther, shouting louder now, his voice shrill as he realised that no-one was coming to help him.

The beast lunged ... and the huge man turned and ran down the empty beach.

The creature waited until his screams had faded before it followed, four broad feet hissing across the loose sand.

Sweat was flowing from the human's body, drops splashing to the sand, leaving a strongly-scented trail the beast could have followed with its eyes closed. Cutting across at an angle, the creature climbed a dune, allowing itself to be silhouetted against the moonlight, knowing the human would see. The beast growled, spurring the human on to greater speed, but it knew he was close to exhaustion.

And then the human stumbled and fell. He rolled onto his back, arms raised to protect his face, and screamed when he saw the beast loom up out of the night.

NO!

The voice was a savage roar in its skull, and the creature paused, shaking its huge head from side to side. Padding forward, the creature sniffed at the man, ignoring his feeble attempts to beat it away. The air was full of his fear, pure and strong ... but there was something else, a softer scent, delicate, different. The scent of a human female. His mate? Not one female scent, but two, the second one alike and yet different, younger. The human's mate, and his daughter.

The beast hesitated, images of a father and his daughter ...

And then the night came alive with the roar of the metal beasts. The creature turned. Three of the other humans were bearing down on her, each riding the swift metal beasts, their single eyes dazzling. One of the humans was spinning a metal chain.

With a final savage growl, the creature turned and melted into the night.

Hours later, as the sky began to lighten, the beast returned to the scene. The air was still filled with the odours of sweat and fear. Many humans had been here; there was a smell of gun oil, and some of the creature's paw prints were splashed with a hard white dust.

The hunt was closing in. It was only a matter of time ...

Above, the sky turned slowly from purple to red, the stars winking out one by one as the moon dropped towards the horizon. The creature turned to face the moon, threw back its head and howled.

2

Del Rey Chronicle, **Sunday, 14 August**
WOLF TERRORISES BEACH PARTY

Last night, in the fifteenth sighting this year of the 'Del Rey Beast', a beach party was attacked by what was described as 'a large wolf'. Construction worker Ricky Harding (38), who was partying with a few friends, said that the wolf "just came out of nowhere. Like, one minute we were just sitting there, next thing we were running for our lives." Harding was apparently singled out by the creature. "It was going to eat me, I just know it was," he told this reporter.

The beast was frightened off by Harding's colleagues, though they lost it among the sand dunes near Ree's Point. Officer Marc Noble from the California Highway Patrol was the first officer on the scene, and he said that it was "a miracle no-one was killed."

Officer Noble dismissed recent speculation that the creature was a mountain lion. "We got some good prints in the sand, and I'm confident that the lab will confirm that they do indeed belong to a wolf."

Sheriff Bradley has reiterated his advice concerning the wolf: "If you see this wolf, on no account approach it, no matter how friendly it might seem. Instead, move quickly and quietly away, and report it as soon as possible to the nearest station. The wolf is extremely dangerous, and – though no-one has been hurt yet – we believe that it's only a matter of time before somebody gets killed." The sheriff confirmed that his office would be mounting search parties for the creature. He added that it was unlikely the wolf would be taken alive.

3

SUNLIGHT WOKE HER.

Rachel Stone threw her arm across her eyes and groaned aloud. She knew, by the position of the sun on her face that it was close to noon. Sitting up in the rumpled bed, she held her head in her hands until the pounding headache subsided, then threw her legs over the side of the bed, stood up dizzily, and staggered into the bathroom. Leaning stiff-armed against the sink, she stared into the mirror. Her blond hair was matted close to her skull, and against her unnaturally pale face her eyes were black-rimmed and deep-sunken. The girl grimaced; she looked as if she'd been up all night.

Stepping into the shower, she felt the sand and grit on her bare feet. Raising her hands to her face, she realised that they too were covered in sand. Rachel moaned, and bit her lip.

Again. It had happened again.

The dreams – wild, terrifying dreams – they weren't dreams at all.

Rachel Stone was a werewolf. Last night she had taken the form of a huge wolf and gone hunting on the beach.

Standing in the shower, Rachel examined herself quickly. There were a couple of small scratches on her legs, arms, and across her shoulders. But they had almost completely healed, and would be gone by nightfall.

She showered quickly and went back into the bedroom and pulled the sheets off the bed, shaking out the sand and dirt before stuffing them in the laundry basket. She'd put the sheets through the washer herself.

She dressed in a denim shirt and jeans and padded barefoot down the hall into the kitchen. She expected it to be empty, but Robert, her father, was sitting at the breakfast bar, munching on a dry waffle as he skimmed through one of the Sunday papers.

"Morning, Rachel," Robert muttered, without turning around. "You're up late. I thought you said you were going to take Tin Man out for a gallop this morning."

Rachel sat down opposite him. "I forgot. I'll take him this afternoon."

Tin Man and Scarecrow were Rachel's two horses, four-year-old palominos, gifts from her father. Horses played a large part in the Stone household. Robert owned several stables throughout the world, and was believed to be one of the most successful horse-breeders of the past fifty years. He was certainly one of the richest and best-known.

Rachel poured herself some orange juice and sipped it slowly, grateful for the feeling of the icy liquid sliding down her throat and chilling her stomach. There was a horrible taste in her mouth and she was queasy.

Robert glanced sidelong at his daughter, grey eyes noting her pale face and bloodshot eyes. "What time did you get to bed at last night?"

She shrugged. "Eleven ... something like that. But I

didn't sleep too well," she added. "It was really hot."

"You sure you weren't watching the horror show on Late-Nite TV?"

"No, Dad, I wasn't."

Robert Stone looked unconvinced. He raised his paper and snapped it open, looking for the financial pages.

Rachel saw the headline "Wolf Terrorises ..." and leaned across the breakfast bar to peer at it more closely.

Her father ruffled the paper in annoyance. "Rachel, you know I hate it when people read over my shoulder."

She smiled. "Sorry, Dad. Anyway, it's not over your shoulder." She paused. "I see the wolf attacked again."

He nodded, and folded the paper to read the article. "Yup. No injuries, though I can't see why not. It chased a bunch of low-lifes around the beach." He sighed. "I wish they'd catch that thing. It must be nearly a year since the first attack."

"Ten months," Rachel said automatically.

"Whatever. I hate the thought that it might try to get in here. It could attack the horses. I think I'll have to beef up security; electric fences, that kind of thing. I've even been thinking about hiring a professional tracker."

Rachel dipped her head so that her father couldn't see her expression. Extra security would make it much more difficult to get back into the house. She stared gloomily into her glass of orange juice. It was bad enough waking up naked in her bedroom, covered in dirt and barely remembering the previous night, but if she were found asleep in the grounds of the house, or, worse still, if she were seen prowling around the grounds in her wolf-state, someone would be certain to shoot her.

Rachel finished her juice and strode out into the enclosed garden, breathing in the rich odours of orchids and damp earth and the fainter tang of the salt sea. She walked on damp flagstones to the patch of earth directly below her window.

Pressed into the soft earth was a wolf-print. There was another smudged impression on the windowsill. Proof that the beast had gone into her bedroom ... and then, what had happened then?

Then it had changed back into a teenage girl.

Rachel grimaced. I am a werewolf.

There were times when she could almost ignore the curse, during the middle of the month when the moon was dark, or still only growing. Then, she could almost dismiss the idea as a crazy nightmare, brought on by too many late-night horror movies, too many bad horror novels. But in the last days before the moon grew full, she could feel the changes beginning to work deep in her body and she knew that it was no dream ... the nightmare was real.

And on the nights of the full moon, her voice would grow deep, tufts of hair would sprout all over her body, her limbs would contract and shorten while her spine lengthened ... Then Rachel Stone's thoughts and mind would be buried beneath an older mind, a wild, primitive intelligence, savage and primal, something that lived for the chase and the kill.

She had not always been this way. But for the past ten months – ever since she returned from Ireland – the were-curse had taken over and reshaped her body.

It had begun in Ireland the previous autumn, with Seasonstown House ...

Robert Stone had snapped up the chance to buy a crumbling old mansion and its stables in the Curragh, the horse-breeding centre of Ireland. Robert had always wanted to own stables in Ireland and planned on developing Seasonstown into an enormous American-style stud farm.

But there was more to Seasonstown House than he had bargained for. When Robert, his wife Elizabeth, and Rachel had arrived at the house for a holiday, they suddenly found themselves thrown into a nightmare of vicious attacks and incredible violence. Seasonstown House was at the heart of an ancient and terrible curse. The evil Clan of Natalis who had once occupied the land had been cursed for their sins to spend their days as lycanthropes – werewolves. But their plan to pass on their curse to the Stones had been foiled by Madoc, one of the clan.

Rachel's memories of the last terrible night, when Seasonstown House burned to the ground, were vague and disjointed. She knew that the terrible clan and their foul leader, Piers de Courtney, had been destroyed, and she vaguely remembered Madoc, then in his wolf shape, dragging her out of the burning building, saving her life.

She hadn't realised – then – that his teeth had sunk into her flesh. But a month later, when the full moon rose over her home in California, Rachel Stone had turned into a werewolf.

Those first few days had been terrifying. A nightmare of images, impressions, scents and sounds.

The change from human to wolf was still a frightening, excruciatingly painful experience, but in the last few months Rachel had discovered another aspect of her wolf form which was even more disturbing. She was enjoying it. She felt free. Alive. There were even times when she found herself looking forward to the full moon.

So far, no-one even suspected a connection between herself and the wolf, though to Rachel it seemed almost transparently obvious: the wolf had appeared immediately after the family had returned from Ireland.

The wolf's first appearances in the small seaside town had been dismissed as nothing more than mistaken identity: a big dog that looked vaguely wolf-like. But with the continued appearances of the wolf, the story was impossible to dismiss. Experts were brought in to prove how scavengers, like wolves and bears, were being lured to towns by the destruction of their natural environment and the encroachment of the towns into their natural hunting grounds. When a television crew had captured a few seconds of blurry video of the wolf it confirmed what the local people had claimed all along: a huge wolf *was* prowling the town. Local businessmen – including Rachel's father – had put up an award, and hunting parties armed with rifles and high-powered hunting bows had swarmed into the town .... luckily they had come at the dark of the moon. They had departed two days before the full moon rose in the sky and the wolf stalked the streets.

It had been a close call. These men were professional hunters and trackers. And they would be back. Rachel knew that sooner or later – probably sooner – she would be caught. And what then? If she was shot would she turn back into her human form?

She had to get rid of the curse.

And she had to do it before she killed someone – or was killed.

But the only person who could help her was Madoc ... and that meant returning to Ireland.

4

RACHEL STONE TOOK A DEEP BREATH, but kept her face expressionless. She was pinning so much on this moment. Standing beside her palomino gelding, Tin Man, she tried to keep from fidgeting and adding to his nervousness. She could tell that the horse was already affected by the rising tension in the crowd.

She had to win this competition; she simply had to. It would give her the chance to return to Ireland without her parents. It would give her a chance to find Madoc.

Young riders from all across the United States had entered the American Horse Show Association's Junior Medal competition, which was the ultimate national test of horsemanship over fences. Last week Rachel had made it through to the top five, proving herself one of the best young riders in the country. But only winning the final round mattered to her. The winner alone would be awarded a trip to the Royal Dublin Horse Show as a special guest of the AHSA.

Today, the final day of the competition, the first three finalists had all made mistakes. Riding fourth, Rachel was exultant when she had a clear round, convinced that she'd won ... until a girl even younger than Rachel had put in another beautifully ridden clear round. It would be decided in another round, this time against the clock.

Rachel patted Tin Man gently, glancing sidelong at

the other girl who was chatting easily with her mother.

The loudspeakers popped and whined. A rawboned woman whose skin was tanned the colour of old leather stood up and tapped at the microphone. She smiled with impossibly perfect teeth at the booming sound it created. "The course will be changed and Rachel Stone on Tin Man and Imelda Rafton on Warrior will ride again," she announced. "Miss Stone will ride first."

Rachel listened carefully while a new course was announced, then she and Imelda, standing shoulder to shoulder but not looking at one another, studied it carefully. When she was sure she had the course memorised, Rachel led Tin Man to the in-gate. She sat straight and proud in the saddle, hands low, heels down, elbows bent at just the proper angle.

When the gate swung open she trotted into the arena, circling to settle Tin Man for the job ahead. Meanwhile her eyes searched for her parents in the crowd. She spotted them in the front of the stand, watching her closely. They were experienced enough not to wave, but she could tell by her father's tight smile and her mother's curt nod that they shared her tension.

A bell rang and Rachel cantered Tin Man towards the first fence, a simple post and rail.

The gelding cleared it easily, muscles bunching then releasing in a flowing jump. Keeping control was important now, she must count the strides in her head to get him right at the next fence. The new course was a figure eight with tight turns. The wall was the trickiest

– one had to approach it at a difficult angle for such a solid-looking fence. A horse could easily refuse there. But Tin Man sailed over, and Rachel breathed a sigh of relief. They were going well.

As they neared the end of the course, however, the palomino tugged at the reins, wanting his head. She drew him back carefully, not wanting to spoil his stride. Gather him, gather him ... now forward, into the final combination of three obstacles in a row.

As they cantered down to the combination, Rachel sensed something was wrong. Tin Man had flattened out, he was covering too much ground and they would come in too close for the take-off.

His hind legs rattled the top pole. Rachel did not dare unbalance him by looking around to see if it had fallen. She tried to gather him in time for the second fence of the combination, but he hit this one hard, knocking it down with a clatter.

Four faults at least, she thought with a sinking heart. Or eight if the first one's down.

The day was very hot and they had already jumped a course. She could feel that Tin Man was tired. "Come on, boy! Please!" she urged him under her breath. Using all her skill, she steadied him with her hands and legs. He responded with a mighty effort, rising at the last fence. This time, this final time when it mattered the most, the big golden horse jumped perfectly.

Only when she heard the crowd cheering did Rachel realise she'd been holding her breath.

She reined Tin Man in and trotted him towards the

out-gate as the announcer's voice came booming over the loud speaker. "Four faults for Rachel Stone and Tin Man. Time: 34.68."

Rachel reached down to pat her horse's shoulder gratefully. "Well done, boy! I only hope it's good enough."

Imelda Rafton trotted in on her black mare, Warrior, as Rachel left the ring. The younger girl was sitting on her mount with absolute arrogance.

Rachel swiftly dismounted, ran up the stirrups and loosened Tin Man's girth. Then she stayed beside the arena, watching with growing fear as Imelda and Warrior cantered around the course, clearing every obstacle with precision. Horse and rider were in perfect harmony. Rachel glanced across to where her father was sitting. He was watching the black horse intently. The mare had a reputation for being temperamental, but she had fine bloodlines. Rachel knew her father had wanted to buy Warrior for his own stables.

Imelda also cleared the wall without any problem, but then the young girl turned her horse too sharply. The black mare's hind legs scrabbled desperately as she nearly fell. Warrior cantered on, but she was obviously shaken.

Imelda sat deep and shortened her reins. The black mare recovered enough to take the next jump faultlessly, and landed in stride for the combination. The three fences in a row were designed to be jumped bounce, bounce, bounce. If you got into it right it was easy.

23

Rachel groaned and turned away. Imelda would not make the same mistake she had. It was all over.

I've just lost my chance of getting back to Ireland, Rachel told herself. My only chance of finding a cure.

And then the crowd moaned.

Rachel turned back to the arena. For some reason Warrior had lost her forward impulsion and Imelda seemed unable to correct the error in time. The black mare made no attempt to jump but crashed into the first fence of the combination, demolishing it.

Rachel stared in disbelief as the bars seemed to fall in slow motion.

Imelda trotted Warrior around to try to regain control, but the horse looked nervous and edgy. Sweat on her glistening black neck was carved to white foam by the reins. As the fence was swiftly reset, the mare danced sideways. When Imelda tried to take the combination again, the mare reared. Imelda circled the mare again and made a final attempt at the fence. But Warrior refused.

The steward's whistle blew, signalling that Imelda was eliminated.

Rachel buried her face in Tin Man's creamy white mane so that no-one could see her tears. She had won after all. She was on her way to Ireland.

5

RACHEL STONE WAS A WOLF AGAIN. But as a werewolf she retained much of her human intellect, she could think like a person.

She was racing through the undergrowth of a dense forest. It was early morning and the ground was damp after a rainstorm, the bushes she crashed through exploding water droplets, splashing onto her pelt, leaving a clear trail for the hunters to follow.

The hunters.

She could hear them behind her, breathing hard, blundering through the forest, coming closer.

Closer.

In her wolf-state, Rachel's senses were acute. She could hear everything the hunters said, could understand their whispered plans to trap her. They were going to try and come at her from all sides at once.

She stopped running suddenly, strong black claws slipping on the moist leaves, then turned her head and breathed deeply, tasting the forest odour, identifying and isolating the odour of men.

The hunters were all middle-aged men, carrying shotguns and knives. One of them was wounded and limping badly. Rachel could smell the blood on his leg, the copper-like scent mixed with the sharp odour of the antiseptic ointment he'd splashed over the wound.

There were other smells too: alcohol and tobacco being the strongest, mingled with eight different aftershave lotions and deodorants. Although she could not smile, Rachel's jaws gaped in a wolfish imitation of a grin. These men had probably spent a year's salary on a camper – which came complete with microwave oven and colour TV – camouflage clothes and cam paint. They hoped these expensive toys would make them self-sufficient and invisible as they 'got back to nature'.

Rachel pricked up her ears, listening carefully: the hunter with the limp seemed to be the best bet. The others had formed a wide circle around her and were closing in, but the wounded man would be easy to get past. She moved carefully towards him, belly low to the ground, hiding herself in the bushes until she caught sight of his green-splotched khaki jacket. He wore a baseball cap pushed back on his head, and carried a hunting rifle casually in his left hand. He seemed exhausted, leaning back against a tree to catch his breath, sweat glistening on his face.

Rachel looked at the hunter with huge unblinking eyes. His right arm and leg were soaked with blood and the fabric of his shirt was hanging open in four long strips.

Did I do that, Rachel wondered? Is that why they're hunting me?

But she couldn't remember.

She never truly remembered what it was like in the wolf-state. Her memories were fragmentary, vague, dreamlike. In the days following her beast-state, she always watched the news and read the papers, terrified that she was going to come across a story about a body being found, a body that had been savaged by a wolf.

So far, she hadn't bitten anyone. So far.

But how long could that last? She had the impression that every time she took on her wolf state she became more and more savage, and the tiny voice of the girl Rachel Stone was slowly being swallowed up by the beast.

The hunter pushed himself away from the tree and marched towards her.

Rachel froze. She couldn't get out of the way without making noise, and if she turned and ran, then he would lift his rifle and fire. He couldn't possibly miss from this distance. There was only one other option: she had to attack him. If she leapt straight for his throat he wouldn't have enough time to bring up the gun. But just attacking him wasn't enough: she had to kill him, quickly and silently, so that he wouldn't have time to warn the others. It was her only way out.

To survive, she had to kill. She had to become the beast. And once that happened, there was no turning back; once she had killed and tasted human blood she would never be able to become human again.

The hunter stepped up to her, looming over her. He bared his teeth in a savage smile and said, "Would you like a pillow?"

Rachel came fully awake. A heavily-made-up stewardess was beaming down at her. "Would you like a pillow?" the stewardess repeated. "It would be a lot more comfortable than sleeping on your neighbour's shoulder."

Rachel blushed and turned to the old man who was sitting next to her in the window seat. It was the wounded hunter from her dreams. "Oh, I'm so sorry. I didn't realise ..."

The old man smiled. "That's okay, honey. You weren't bothering me."

The stewardess offered the pillow again. Rachel shook her head. "No, I'm fine, really."

"Maybe something to drink?"

"Yes please, coke ... no, tea would be lovely."

"I'd like some tea too, " the old man said.

The stewardess flashed her artificial smile again, and marched off down the aisle. Rachel smothered a yawn and glanced at her watch. It was four o'clock in the morning. Only another couple of hours before they landed in Dublin.

"Nightmare?" the old man asked. "You were twitching and jumping around. Whatever you were dreaming about must have been pretty scary."

By now, Rachel could only barely remember her dream, images and impressions slipping away. Something about being hunted, she knew, but that was all. She shrugged. "I'm not sure. I'm sorry if I woke you," she added.

"You didn't wake me. I couldn't sleep. Are you nervous about flying?" the old man asked, turning to smile at her. "Is this your first time on a plane?" he inquired kindly.

Rachel noticed that the man was gripping the armrests. He was at least seventy, almost completely bald, clean-shaven, but with thick white eyebrows that dominated his face. He seemed eager to talk ... and she thought she knew why. "No," she answered. "I've flown loads of times. What about you?"

He grimaced. "First time. I've been saving all my life to go back home to Ireland."

"I don't hear any Irish accent?" Rachel said.

"I've lived in LA since the end of the war. I don't suppose there's much of an accent left."

Rachel nodded automatically, although she wasn't sure which war he was talking about. Vietnam? Korea? Surely not the Second World War? She looked at him again, and realised he might just be old enough.

"Is this your first visit?" he asked.

"My second. I was in Ireland late last year."

"Did you like it?"

"I loved it," she lied easily.

The old man nodded. "I'm seventy-seven this year. I thought I should go home, see the old sod before I die." He smiled to take the sting out of his words.

Rachel shuddered. The words sounded ominous.

6

THE BOY STIRRED UNEASILY IN HIS SLEEP.

Something was wrong, something was very wrong.

He was standing in a tunnel facing a white spot of light, but the light was growing as it raced towards him.

Someone was coming ... someone he knew.

The boy jerked backwards with a grunt, eyes blazing in the gloom, every sense alert. The walls and ceiling of his tiny bedroom were splashed with amber and crimson from the street lights which shone through the bare windows. When he was confident that the room was empty he sat up, breathing deeply, calming himself. He brought his clenched fists up level with his face and slowly opened them. His long nails had scored perfect half-circles into the flesh of his palms.

Someone was coming.

Who?

He reached out with his thoughts and allowed them to soar, permitting his acute senses to take control. Images from his dreams came flooding back.

Fire.

He was seeing fire. Dancing flames, and in the heart of the flames, the face of a girl – blond, blue-eyed – a face he knew. A face he hadn't thought about for a long time.

The American girl, Rachel Stone.

But why should he be thinking about her now?

Danger coming.

Madoc sighed deeply. Climbing out of bed, he crossed to the window and stared out into the night, the street lights washing his face in amber and shadow.

Rachel Stone was coming back to Ireland.

Madoc's lips pulled back from his teeth in a savage smile, and for an instant – a single instant – the face of a beast was reflected in the dirty glass. The boy shuddered and the image vanished. Climbing back into the narrow bed he pulled the single blanket over his shoulders. But he didn't get to sleep again that night.

A huge, misshapen figure crouched low over the pool and slowly stirred it with a gnarled oak stick. Here, deep in the heart of the cave, there was little light, but the pool emitted a glow of its own – ice-blue, purple-black – not enough to illuminate the cave, but enough to lend the figure shape and substance. A large black raven jumped from the figure's shoulder to the ground, and darted after a beetle.

She was coming.

He could sense the approach of the shapechanger. A female. And she was powerful, so powerful, with the ancient magic strong in her veins. She was special, so special: she was untainted by another's blood. She had yet to make her first kill.

The figure stirred the pool a second time, digging the stick deeply. Oily ripples broke up the scum on the surface, cracking it in a crazy pattern. But when the liquid had settled, it showed the face of a girl – fourteen, fifteen, perhaps sixteen summers – with shoulder-length blond hair and clear blue eyes ...

The face of the shapechanger.

The figure stared at that face for a long time until the image faded and the pool clouded over once more.

He nodded. The girl was perfect! A powerful shapechanger, she would be very useful, very useful indeed. Looking at her face had given him a *sense* of her. She was headstrong, and brave, and he knew she would still think of herself as human, even though she had moved beyond that despicable race.

The figure tossed the stick aside and straightened, joints popping and cracking, testimony to extreme age. He had waited a long time for this moment, grown old waiting for the girl or someone like her ... no, not someone *like* her. He had grown ancient waiting for her.

The girl had great potential, but was naive, innocent. She knew nothing of the ancient ways. *Nothing!* She thought she had learned everything about the shapechangers from the Clan of Natalis, but they were nothing. A clan of fools. Dangerous, to be sure, but fools nevertheless.

He knew why she was coming back to Ireland. She feared the were-change, and wanted to be rid of it. He knew what she would do: she would try to contact the last of the Clan of Natalis, seeking his aid. But that must not happen. No-one must get to her before he had made her an offer of his own. He would lift the were-curse from her ... and the price would not be too high.

Her blood.

Her soul.

RACHEL WAITED UNTIL THE BELLBOY had left the room and then collapsed on the huge double bed. She was exhausted, but knew if she slept now, she'd wake up in the afternoon and be awake for the rest of the night. She needed to get her body in sync with Irish time. Rolling over, she picked up the phone, pressed 9 to get an outside line, then the international code, the area code, and her home number.

The distant phone rang three times before it was picked up. Her mother's voice sounded tiny and lost. "Hello?"

"Mom? It's me! I'm in the hotel."

Elizabeth Stone let out a sigh of relief. "Thank God! I was beginning to get worried! Is everything all right? Were you met at the airport?"

"Sure. Mister Stafford was waiting for me. I recognised him from Dad's description, and he knew me from the photograph Dad had faxed him. He said he'll give me a lift back to the airport when I go back to the States."

"I'm relieved. You have to promise me you'll be careful. You know I'm still not happy about you going to Ireland on your own."

"Mom, it's too late now. I'm already here. Besides, the American Olympic Team is here too, remember, and their *chef d'equipe* is supposed to look out for me. It's all arranged."

"I know." Elizabeth Stone sighed theatrically. "You just be careful. Remember what happened last year at Seasonstown House?"

Rachel raised her eyes to the ceiling. "How could I forget? Mom, I *knew* you were going to bring that up! It's okay, *really*. We've been over this a hundred times already. I'll only be here for a week. What could happen to me in a week? Besides, the hotel is only a couple of hundred yards from the Royal Dublin showgrounds, and it's right in the heart of the city."

"You'll phone us every day, right?"

"Sure."

"What time is it over there?"

"It's ten in the morning," Rachel said with a glance at the bedside clock.

"It's not even daylight yet here."

"I'm sorry, Mom, I didn't realise it was so early. I'll try and phone at a reasonable time in future."

"Phone anytime," Elizabeth Stone insisted. "Have you been in touch with Margaret yet?" Margaret Chapman was an old friend of Rachel's mother. She was currently holidaying in Ireland, and had promised to check up on Rachel from time to time.

"Not yet, Mom," Rachel said. "I'll phone her before I go to sleep this afternoon."

"All right ..." She paused. "Rachel, don't do anything stupid, eh? You know, when I was your age ..." she began.

"Mom, when you were my age you'd already spent two summers picking grapes in France! And you were

34

on your own for two *months* each time! I'll be fine. Stop worrying."

"Send me a postcard," Elizabeth said quickly and rang off before her daughter could hear the tears in her voice.

Rachel replaced the phone on the cradle and smiled ruefully. After what had happened in Seasonstown House she couldn't blame her mother for being worried. Her parents wanted to protect her from harm, but in reality it was far too late for that. She had already been harmed in a way they could never understand.

She lay back on the pillow, her hands locked behind her head and stared at the ceiling ...

... and woke up three hours later.

Rolling over, she glanced at the clock ... and went back to sleep.

8

RACHEL WOKE WITH THE SUN IN HER EYES. She lay in bed and listened to churchbells pealing out across the city, and realised that it was a Sunday morning. When she looked at the clock, she discovered it was eight o'clock. She had slept for nearly nineteen hours. Aching muscles protested as she sat up and she groaned aloud. However, she knew from experience that the feeling would pass after she had showered and had breakfast.

She was carefully picking through an enormous Irish breakfast half an hour later when a tall, slim, elegant woman entered the restaurant and moved towards her table.

"Rachel Stone?"

"Yes?" Rachel looked up in surprise, then said, "You must be Margaret Chapman ... Mrs Chapman."

"I'm Margaret Chapman." The woman sat down opposite her.

"Mom phoned?" Rachel guessed.

Margaret Chapman smiled. "She did. She was worried about you."

A young waitress appeared and Margaret ordered coffee. Rachel glanced over the rim of her own cup at the woman. She was younger than Rachel had first thought – early twenties – with cold grey eyes dominating her hard-boned face. Her blond hair had been styled to look unstyled.

"I got into Dublin late last night," Margaret Chapman said, "and I unfortunately have to fly out again tomorrow afternoon, so I thought I'd better call on you today."

"You're very kind."

Margaret's coffee arrived. "Did you have any plans? Was there anything you particularly wanted to see?"

Rachel shook her head. "I hadn't really thought about it. I'd like to look around, I suppose. I didn't have a chance to do much sightseeing last year," she added.

"Your mother told me," Margaret said. "It sounded like a horrible experience."

"It was," Rachel said feelingly.

"I'm surprised you came back."

Rachel finished the last of her tea. I had no choice, she thought. I had to come back.

Rachel dropped her sunglasses over her eyes as they stepped out into the brilliant morning sunshine. She had brought a sweatshirt – she remembered from last year how cold it could get in Ireland – but after a few minutes she was forced to take it off and tie it around her shoulders.

Margaret and Rachel walked down towards the RDS, passing the American Embassy on the right. "That's where to go if there's any trouble," Margaret remarked, nodding in the direction of the large round building. "Pretty ugly, though, isn't it?"

Rachel shrugged. "I don't know. It certainly stands out among all these old houses."

"Most of them are mid- to late-nineteenth century," Margaret explained, "built when Ireland was under British rule. From what I understand, this area – Ballsbridge it's called – was where a lot of the landlords used to live, while their tenants were starving to death on tiny farms down the country." She shook her head. "It's ironic, because nowadays most of these houses have been chopped up into flats and bedsits. Now the landlords live in the country."

"How do you know so much about Irish history?" Rachel wondered. "Have you lived here long?"

"I was born here," the older woman replied, "but my family moved to the States while I was still a small child. My older sister and your mother were in college together. Your mother used to baby-sit me," she grinned.

And now you're baby-sitting me, Rachel thought, but said nothing.

They crossed over the bridge and came to a pub called The Horse Show House. Rachel blinked in sur- prise at the name, then looked across the road to see the magnificent buildings of the Royal Dublin Society. Her hotel was indeed very close to the showgrounds.

"That's where you'll be most of the time, I suppose," Margaret said. "Have you any idea what you'll be doing? Your mother wasn't sure. She said you won some competition just to be here."

"I don't know yet," Rachel said. "I'm not going to be in any jumping classes, but I'll be introduced as the winner of the American Junior Medal. It's sort of a good will exercise on behalf of the American Horse Shows Association. I'll be given a horse to ride and do a lap of honour. And I think I'm supposed to give interviews to the local papers."

"What sort of horses do you have at home?"

"Two palominos. I call them Tin Man and Scarecrow, after ..."

"After *The Wizard of Oz*, by L. Frank Baum!" Margaret interrupted delightedly. "They're some of my favourite books!"

"Mine too," said Rachel, though she'd never read the books, only seen the film with Judy Garland.

"There's a funny story about the *Wizard of Oz*," Margaret told her. "Apparently, when the guy who was playing the Wizard in the film – I think his name was Frank Morgan – was in the costume department trying to find something to wear for his part as the doctor, he found an old overcoat tossed in a corner. He pulled the coat on and discovered a book in one of the pockets. But what was really strange was that it was L. Frank Baum's personal copy of the book, and the coat belonged to the author too. Yet no-one ever discovered how it had got there."

Rachel grinned. "Sounds like a Hollywood story."

"Apparently it's true," Margaret said, with wide-eyed innocence. Rachel wasn't sure if she was joking with her or not.

They crossed the road and walked past the RDS, then turned to the right, enjoying the morning air and sunshine. Although the road was wide, there was surprisingly little traffic. The houses were large and elegant with big, well-tended gardens and fine old trees.

"I thought we were close to the city," Rachel said.

"We are. The city centre is only a couple of kilometres from where we're standing."

"But it seems so peaceful here, like being in the country."

"That," Margaret explained, "is because it's Sunday morning. Tomorrow morning this road will be solid with traffic."

They walked on in silence for a time. Then Rachel asked, "What do you do for a living?"

"I scout locations for movies. I travel all over the world looking for just the right site for a scene, or an entire film. I found a very dramatic ruined castle for the last Bond movie," she added proudly. "We filmed that bit here in Ireland."

"It must be a fascinating job. I'll bet you get to meet a lot of big stars."

Margaret nodded. "I've met them all. On Friday, for example, I had lunch with Daniel –" She stopped when Rachel grabbed her arm. "What?"

The girl swallowed. She was turning her head from side to side. "Did you hear that?"

"Hear what?"

"It sounded like a dog howling."

"I didn't hear anything." Margaret tilted her head to one side, listening. "No. Nothing like that at all."

"I hear it," Rachel insisted, staring straight ahead

towards a bend in the road. Then she closed her eyes and concentrated. It was a dog, a large dog; she could hear its laboured breathing and the sound of its paws on the pavement. The beast was emitting a low keening sound, as though it were terrified, but at the same time it was growling as if it were ready to fight.

And it was definitely coming closer.

"Run!" Rachel said, tugging at Margaret's arm. "Come on! Run!"

Margaret hesitated. "It's only a dog."

Rachel knew that some dogs went into a frenzy if they got the scent of a wolf. Was it possible her wolf odour was now affecting her human state? If the dog was reacting to it, it could be very dangerous. As a werewolf she would have no trouble outrunning any dog, but like this ...

"Run!" she screamed, dropping Margaret's arm and stepping back.

Margaret stood still for a few seconds, unsure what to do. When a large German Shepherd rounded the corner, snarling in fury, she stiffened in fright. But the dog ignored her and hurtled towards Rachel with every hair on its neck bristling.

The girl ran. She had to lead the animal away from the woman, and she had to lure it to a place where she could deal with it. She could hear its claws scrabbling on the pavement only a few yards behind her.

I am not afraid, she tried to tell herself. The dog is nothing. I am much more powerful; I *can* be much more powerful.

She turned and glared unblinkingly at the dog. Slowly, she drew her lips back from her teeth.

The dog advanced towards her stiff-legged, refusing to be intimidated. Its growls became deeper, more angry.

Rachel's nerve broke and she opened her mouth to scream ... but the only sound that came out was a growl infinitely more chilling than that of the dog.

The German Shepherd stopped in its tracks and stared at her.

She growled again.

The dog gave a frightened yelp and backed up, then turned and fled.

Rachel drew a deep, shuddering breath. She spread her fingers and looked at her hands, then felt her face. She was not in the process of a change, there was no full moon. Her face was still the face she knew.

Yet, somehow, she had drawn on her animal half. She had used that energy deliberately, effortlessly. The dog had recognised it and panicked.

But she was frightened too, and not by her near escape.

"What's happening to me?" she asked herself, her voice nothing more than a hoarse whisper.

The werewolf spell was growing stronger she realised, with a thrill of horror.

She turned back the way she had come, rounded the corner and ran straight into Margaret Chapman. Both women screamed.

9

RACHEL BREATHED DEEPLY, ENJOYING the rich odours of horse and leather. It was a smell she had grown up with and it always brought happy memories. She was wandering through the RDS wearing her boots and jodhpurs, with a plastic identity tag around her neck, looking for someone who knew what she was supposed to be doing.

Although she had flown to Ireland on the same plane as some of the American Olympic Team, she did not really know them. And now that they were at the show they were too busy to talk to her. There was an AHSA representative here too, but she had not yet found that person. A look at the day's schedule told her that her first lap of honour was scheduled at eleven that morning. But where was the horse the AHSA had arranged for her to ride?

She entered the stabling area, which was quiet now that all the excitement was going on in the arenas beyond. She spotted a portly, middle-aged groom sitting on a tack chest, reading a newspaper.

"Hi, I'm Rachel Stone. I don't suppose –"

"Of course! The American lass! We've been looking for you. Thought we'd have to send out a search party. I understand you need a horse to ride, eh? Come with me, then, Rachel. We've one put aside for you." He had a very strong Irish accent, and spoke far too quickly for Rachel to understand, but she managed to decipher enough words to catch his meaning.

Rachel followed him down a long row of loose boxes. "I've been here all morning, but everyone seemed far too busy. I thought I'd make myself scarce until things settled down."

"Very sensible," he nodded. He opened one of the boxes and led out a large bay pony. "This is Rob," the groom said. "Now, did they teach you anything about horses in America?"

"A little," Rachel replied.

"Well, I'll give you one piece of advice. Keep to his side, all right? The front end bites and the other end does terrible things altogether."

"Don't worry, I've seen one or two horses in my time," Rachel assured the man. She did not like being patronised just because she was an American.

The man slapped the pony on the flank. "Be good to her, boy. We'd like to be able to send all of her home in the one package."

Rob whickered and bowed his head, almost as if he was acknowledging the joke.

"Will you need a hand with the saddle?"

"I can manage. Really," Rachel insisted.

"Well, I'm here if you need anything," the old man said dubiously, looking at her as if he was not quite sure she would be able even to lift the saddle.

She picked up the saddle and heaved it onto the pony's back. While she worked, she could feel eyes on the back of her neck. She thought the groom was willing her to make a mistake so he could step in and show her how it was done. But she didn't make a mistake.

Nor was he watching.

Keeping to the shadows on the roof of one of the buildings, two other figures *were* watching Rachel – intently. Their eyes were a greenish yellow, with vertical slits for pupils. They stared unblinkingly at the girl, then one turned to the other and nodded. The second figure hissed gently. The scent of wolf was strong in the air. There was no mistake. This was the girl. They crouched deeper in the shadows, and waited.

Rachel reined Rob to a stop, and dipped her head slightly to acknowledge the applause from the crowd. She was almost disappointed. The lap of honour had been no more than a gallop around the main arena; she was not even allowed to jump any of the obstacles. The pony was very nappy, however, bucking at first and then trying to turn and head back towards the stable. But Rachel managed him with practised skill. This pleased the crowd. The announcer had spent more time telling everyone about Rachel than she had spent actually riding. Still, she told herself, maybe they'll have something more for me to do in the afternoon.

She slid from the saddle and led Rob back towards the stables. The stout groom met her on the way. "You did well," he said, sounding surprised.

"Were you watching?"

"I was indeed. Thought you might have a wee bit of trouble with old Rob, actually. Ponies can be difficult, you know. Stubborn. Minds of their own. And Rob here is almost as big as a horse, with a horse's strength but a pony's cunning. You handled him well, though."

Rachel blushed. "Thanks. You're very kind."

He shook his head. "No, don't thank me for telling the truth. You're a winner, Miss Rachel, there's no doubt. At least, you're a potential winner. Do you know the difference?"

Rachel shook her head. "I'm not sure. Tell me."

He led the horse inside the stall, fingers already busy with the buckles and straps. "There are two types of people in this business, Miss Rachel. Those who do, and those who talk about it. I've seen boys and girls your age who are just as skilful as you are, but most of them never get anywhere. And that's because they try to run before they can walk. You know what I mean?"

"I think so. People tell them they're good, and they believe it and think that they can stop trying." She was recalling Imelda as she spoke.

"Right. Never stop trying, Miss Rachel."

When Rob had been rubbed down, Rachel left the stables and wandered back to the main hall. She noticed Margaret waiting by a pillar. The two recognised one another simultaneously and waved.

"You were very good, absolutely marvellous!" the older woman gushed. "Do you think you'll ever go professional?"

"Maybe," said Rachel. "I'd like to, but it all depends on what happens in the next few years. College is the most important thing. Dad said that I can do whatever I like with my life, as long as I get a good education."

"He's right of course." Margaret glanced at the oversized Swatch watch on her wrist. "What are your plans for this afternoon?"

"I want to get back to the hotel and shower before I appear again. I ride twice each day, you know. It's very little, really – somehow I thought there would be more. But ... what time is your flight?"

"Three-fifteen. I really should be making a move. But I wanted to see you first."

"Thanks for everything, Margaret."

"Not at all. I enjoyed it."

"Even if we gave each other a fright?" Rachel teased. She could laugh about it now.

Margaret laughed too. "Silly, wasn't it? Listen to me – I'll be back in Dublin later in the week. I'll call. We could have dinner; I know a lovely little restaurant on the north side of the city."

"Sure, that would be great!"

The older woman kissed Rachel quickly on the cheeks, then turned and walked away, melting into the crowd without a backward glance. The girl got the distinct impression that the woman was relieved that she'd completed a chore. Rachel knew Margaret would not call for dinner. Then she stopped: how could she possibly know that?

The answer was instinctive. Her senses were becoming more acute. She disliked Margaret in the same way that a dog takes a dislike to a person. It senses something about them, a combination of odour and instinct.

Rachel's beast nature was coming to the fore.

The two figures followed at a distance, keeping to the rooftops, flowing with the shadows. Watching. Waiting. They had watched the two women talking, and the taller of the watchers hissed in alarm when the older woman reached to kiss the girl. They'd been told the girl would be alone.

They relaxed when the woman walked away.

"Now?" the tall one hissed.

"This is not the time," the second, smaller creature whispered. "We must wait until she is alone, until she is vulnerable, before we take her."

"We must not fail," the other replied, still hissing angrily. "The Master said that she is powerful. If she should prove too powerful for us ..."

Its companion gave a short, high-pitched, shrieking laugh. "Too powerful for us? A softskin, unable to control the change, unsure what's happening! She won't stand a chance against us."

"She faced down the canine."

"The dog was a mindless beast. *We* are cunning. We won't fail."

10

RACHEL TURNED OFF THE SHOWER and pulled on one of the hotel's luxuriously fluffy bathrobes. Wrapping a towel around her damp hair, she wandered out into the bedroom and sat down at the dressing table to dry her hair. She picked up the hairdryer ...

Watching.

... and dropped it immediately.

Rachel spun around in the chair and stared out the window. There's something out there, she thought. Something ...

As quickly as it came, the feeling of being watched vanished. She stood up, walked over to the window, parted the curtains and peered out. She could see nothing out of the ordinary. Her room looked out over the back of the hotel into the car park. A blue Volvo estate was manoeuvring into a tight parking spot in the corner: maybe that's what had alerted her acute senses.

She returned to the dressing table and picked up the hairdryer, relieved to find that it was still working. From below she heard the faint scrape of metal, and realised that the Volvo hadn't made it into the space. Then her smile faded. She was listening to a sound from six floors down. What would happen if her senses continued to develop at this rate? She knew humans were capable of perceiving a lot of different sights and sounds and sensations, but that the brain dulled them because it was unable to process the enormous amount of data. Would the sensory overload – the sights, sounds and smells that were normally hidden from humans – prove too much for her? Would they drive her mad?

Rachel turned the hairdryer on full and allowed the blast of hot air to wipe away her thoughts.

It was close to two by the time Rachel returned to the RDS. She waved to the familiar groom, who smiled and nodded back. "You've got Rob again," he called.

Rachel entered Rob's loose box, talking softly so as not to startle the pony. She stopped when she discovered a young man grooming Rob, with his back turned to her.

"Oh! I'm sorry," Rachel said. "I didn't know there was anyone in here. I'm Rachel Stone, I'm here for –"

"I know who you are and why you're here," the young man said rudely. "You should have been able to tell I was here before you even stepped into the stables, Rachel."

The girl stopped, staring at him blankly, but aware that her heart was beginning to pound. Almost unconsciously, her nostrils flared and she caught the faintest hint of ... wolf? "Who are you? Do I know you?"

"You should." He dropped the brush and turned around slowly, then stepped into the light. Sunlight turned red hair gold.

Rachel's mouth dropped open. "Madoc!"

The young man smiled. "It's good to see you, Rachel," he said.

Rachel was shocked. She opened and closed her mouth, but nothing she wanted to say seemed right. Finally, she managed to ask, "How did you know I was here?"

"People like us can sense things." He paused and added with a shy smile, "You should know that by now."

The girl stared at the red-haired boy. He hadn't changed since the last time she'd seen him. He was wearing an old white Aran jumper, badly in need of a wash, and blue jeans faded almost white. His red hair was sticking up all over his head and she could see straw caught in it, as if he had slept in a barn. "I never really got the chance to thank you for saving my life," Rachel said slowly.

Madoc stared at her, green eyes glowing, but made no reply.

She asked him, "Do you know what happened that night?"

"I do know." He took a deep breath. "I passed on the curse to you."

Rachel's eyes brimmed with tears, and she sagged against the door frame. "It's awful, Madoc. I don't seem to have any control over what happens to me. I'm terrified I'll kill someone. And the beast part of me seems to be getting stronger."

Madoc stepped forward and put his arms around her. "I know, I know ... I'm so sorry, Rachel. It's all my fault. But ... " He put his hand under her chin and tilted her face up. "Look at me, Rachel, *listen* to me! You haven't hurt anyone, because you *do* have some control. It might not seem like enough when the moon is full and the beast emerges, but you have to remember that it's a part of you. The wolf isn't a separate animal, it's *you,* all the way through, and if you're the sort of person who won't hurt others, then neither is the wolf."

"I don't want this!" Rachel sobbed. "I came back to get rid of the curse! I want to be totally human again!"

Madoc was silent for a long time. Then, when he finally spoke, his voice was filled with sadness. "I'm sorry, Rachel. It's just not possible."

Rachel pounded her fists against his chest. "It must be!"

"No," he whispered. "There is no cure for this terrible disease."

Rachel pushed away from him. "Then what's going to happen to me?" she demanded. "I'm going to end up killing someone, or getting shot by an eager hunter."

Madoc shook his head. "No, you're not. I can teach you how to control the beast."

That afternoon, Rachel was asked to present awards to some of Ireland's junior riders who were competing at the show. Madoc watched from a distance as she made a graceful little speech about the future of riding. Her own enthusiasm and love for the sport was obvious in her voice, which his keen hearing easily understood.

This is not the time to tell her, he said to himself, but she must know sometime.

He had sensed danger from the moment he became aware that Rachel was coming to Ireland. But the danger wasn't from Rachel herself, but from another. Someone who was so powerful Madoc could only barely grasp the concept.

He was frightened for her, and for himself. Rachel was still unable to control her shape-shifting. She would be all but helpless against someone who was truly experienced.

Yet when Madoc had touched her, and felt her strength flow into him, he had realised for the first time that she was even more powerful than he was. Rachel was a novice, but with great potential. Given time ...

But there was no time, Madoc realised. The others would seek her out and come for her.

He breathed in the warm air, sorting through odours of horse and human, dust and straw, clothing and leather, until he caught the faintest hint of shapechanger.

They had already been here!

The boy bared his teeth in alarm and faded back into the shadows.

Rachel was still shaken from her meeting with Madoc. She'd desperately wanted to see him again, believing he would know some cure, some spell that would reverse the curse. But she should have realised that if he'd known anything like that, he would have used it himself. He'd been her last hope ... and he'd failed.

She walked back to the hotel in a daze. There is no cure, there is no cure, she repeated to herself. I'm stuck like this forever.

Madoc had promised to come to her hotel room later that night and begin her training in the ways of the beast. He could help her control it, but for how long?

She entered the lift and stabbed the number six on the control panel. As the lift rose smoothly, she leaned against the mirrored walls and closed her eyes ... and opened them again almost at once. For an instant, a single instant, she had smelled ... what? Something strange, an alien odour, yet almost familiar.

She was still puzzling over the strange smell when the lift stopped and she stepped out onto the sixth floor. Her room was at the end of the corridor. Suddenly her nostrils flared. The smell was stronger here, sharper. It was like ... like ...

Rachel slid her plastic key into the lock, and the door clicked. She pushed open the door, but it stopped halfway and stuck. Frowning, she pushed harder, hearing something scrape on the floor, and managed to get the door wide enough to squeeze through.

"Oh no!"

The room had been trashed. Her clothes lay scattered everywhere, ripped to shreds. There were deep scratches along the walls, pulling the paper off in ragged strips. Carpet was torn from the floor, the curtains hung limply from a broken curtain rail. The bed had been ripped apart. Stuffing from the mattress littered the room, together with a cloud of feathers from the pillows. Paper was wadded up and tossed about, chairs were overturned.

Heart beating furiously, Rachel stepped through the debris. In the bathroom she saw that the toilet had been smashed and the mirror cracked. All of her toiletries had been hurled to the floor, the bottles broken on the tiles, her perfume mixing with shampoo and talcum powder into a fragrant sludge.

Rachel's first thought was to call the hotel's security, but almost immediately she decided against that. There was only one person she knew who was capable of doing this: Madoc.

"But why?" she asked aloud.

He had done this before. He had destroyed her bedroom and the library in Seasonstown House in one of his attempts to scare Rachel's family away from the house.

But why would he do this? What could it possibly accomplish?

Picking her way back across the ruined room, she hung the DO NOT DISTURB sign on the door and locked it. She hoped Madoc was still in the RDS. She had some questions that needed answers.

11

GETTING BACK INTO THE RDS PROVED surprisingly easy. She simply showed the gatekeeper her laminated ID and said she wanted to check up on her horse.

The competitions were finished for the day and only a scattering of people remained in the grounds, most of them wearing the white coats of the RDS staff. No-one paid her any attention as she walked purposefully across the empty car park, past the old administrative buildings, and into the stable compound.

This was the last place she'd seen Madoc, and she'd got the impression that he was living in the stables. He certainly had the appearance of someone who was living rough, and she suddenly felt guilty because she hadn't even asked him how he'd been getting on since the rest of the Clan of Natalis had been destroyed. What had he been doing in the eight months since the fire? Where had he been living? At least she'd been able to go back to her beautiful home ... but he'd had nothing to go back to.

As she stepped into Rob's stable the pony shied away from her. Rachel spoke softly, murmuring non-sense words, and was holding out her hand to pat him when she stopped, senses suddenly acute.

Someone was coming.

Madoc? No.

She sniffed instinctively, and noticed a faint sour odour beneath the richer scents of horse and stables.

She breathed deeply. The odour was *familiar*...

Rob whickered, becoming even more nervous. And then Rachel suddenly realised that it wasn't she whom he was frightened of, it was whoever was outside.

Rachel pressed back into the shadows, turning her head sideways, pulling her hair away from her ear. She could make out two sets of footsteps. Rubber soles squeaked off the stones. She heard one of them whisper something very softly, the voice not much more than a hiss. The footsteps stopped outside Rob's stable.

Rachel took a few steps back, bringing her hands up in front of her, fingers clawed, unconsciously baring her teeth. A shadow fell across the door, and Rachel crouched, ready to spring ...

Two teenage girls appeared in the doorway. "Hello?" one of them said, her voice trembling slightly as she squinted into the darkness.

Rachel felt a surge of relief. She straightened and stepped forward out of the shadows. Both girls jumped back. "Hi! Sorry, I didn't mean to scare you."

The taller of the girls showed her teeth in a quick smile. "Oh, it's you! We saw someone creeping down around here and thought it was a horse thief or something. You're Rachel Stone, aren't you? The American girl?"

Rachel nodded. "I was just checking up on Rob here." The pony had grown still, but she could feel his muscles trembling beneath his glossy skin. "He seemed very nervous, as if something had frightened him."

"Probably all the noise," said the taller girl.

Rachel looked closely at the pair. They were both lightly built, with closely-cropped black hair. Their faces were clear and pale, with high, prominent cheekbones, slightly tilted green eyes and dark, arched eyebrows. They were dressed alike in black jeans and black polo-neck jumpers, and Rachel guessed they were sisters. "So, you know who I am, who are you?"

"I'm Camille," the taller girl said. "This is Christine. We saw you earlier today. You're very good."

Rachel grinned and shrugged. "It's just a lot of practice. Tell me, how come you two are still here? I thought everyone had gone home."

"We're staying here," Christine said quickly, pointing in the direction of the administration buildings. Her voice was low and hoarse as if her throat had been damaged at one time. "We look after the horses at night. We're pretty good with animals," she added with a sly smile.

Rachel patted Rob again, noting how he seemed to be keeping as far away from the girls as possible, almost as if he was afraid of them. She was aware of a peculiar odour emanating from the girls that was almost – but not quite – a perfume. The smell was sharper, more acidic, like bitter lemons or limes. "Listen, have you seen a boy around here in the last few minutes? About my age, tall, sort of thin, with bright red hair?"

Camille shook her head. "I don't think so."

Christine shrugged. "Red hair? That could be almost half the population of Ireland."

"Dirty jeans, Aran jumper?"

"Still half the population."

They all laughed, the girls smiling, simultaneously almost, but not quite showing their teeth.

"Are you two twins, or what?" Rachel asked.

Christine shook her head. "No."

"Sisters?"

Camille shook her head. "No."

"You're not sisters?" Rachel was astonished. "That's amazing. You look so much alike."

Both girls smiled simultaneously, an act that made Rachel suddenly very nervous.

"Of course we look alike," Christine said. "We ... belong to the same ... clan."

Rachel Stone felt ice settle in the pit of her stomach. She swallowed hard. "Clan?" She was abruptly aware that the two girls were blocking the door.

Christine grinned, showing very prominent incisors. "Oh yes, Rachel, our clan. You know all about clans, don't you? You know about the Clan of Natalis?" Her smile broadened at the look of horror on Rachel's face. "That boy you're looking for, the boy you met today, Madoc – he is Clan Natalis, isn't he?"

"How do you know about that?" Rachel demanded.

Camille hissed. "The Clan Natalis wasn't the only shapechanger clan. It was only a part of the Clan Allta, the were-folk."

"What do you want with me?"

Without answering, Christine leaped. Her teeth were bared and her hands twisted into claws. She caught Rachel with a vicious swipe across her face, sending the American staggering.

When Rachel touched her cheek she felt blood.

Christine laughed, high-pitched and cackling, and then Camille approached. She slashed out with her claws, the blow numbing Rachel's arm. Hissing and screeching, the two girls herded Rachel into a corner of the stable, trapping her. "That was a demonstration of our power. You cannot resist us. You are the dog ... but we are the cat. You must come with us."

The anger began deep in the pit of her stomach. It flowed up through her body, flooding her flesh with heat. She felt the skin draw back over her teeth, and watched as her fingernails visibly extended. Muscles and bones cracked and popped, her spine twisting, throwing her forward into a low crouch. Rachel growled.

"Come with us!" Camille hissed. "We were sent for you. Obey us!"

"Never!" Rachel screamed, her voice deep and angry.

Camille and Christine kept ducking and weaving, dodging from side to side, moving almost too quickly for Rachel to see. She lashed out with her claws at Christine, but the girl nimbly flipped backwards onto her hands, spun in the air, and landed on her feet, snarling.

"It was you two who destroyed my hotel room, wasn't it?" Rachel said. "Not Madoc." For an instant she felt as if she were in a dream – the dream where she was both wolf and human – and then she felt the stickiness on her cheek. This was no dream.

"The dog won't help you now," Camille hissed. "There are two of us, Rachel, and we're part of a clan; *we've* been shapechangers all our lives, *you're* just a novice."

While the girl was speaking, Rachel darted forward and slammed into Christine with her shoulder, while at the same time she lashed out at Camille with her nails. The two cat-girls shrieked and fell back from the fury of the attack. "Cats may be fast, but dogs are stronger," she grunted, sinking her fist into Camille's stomach. She then kicked Christine in the shin, sending her crashing to the ground.

Rachel jumped over the two fallen girls and ran outside.

She stopped half-way across the compound and looked back to the stable. Inside the doorway Christine lay on the ground, clutching her leg and moaning. Camille was crouched protectively over her clan member. Then she lifted her head towards Rachel and spat like an angry cat. She began scrambling along the ground on her hands and knees. As Rachel watched, the girl's body began shuddering, twisting, trembling. Her limbs became shorter, more muscular. Hair sprouted, covering her face in a fine fur, while her entire body lengthened, stretching and tearing her human clothing.

It took less than a dozen heartbeats to change the girl into a black panther. With a roar, the beast burst out of

61

the stables. Keeping its distance from Rachel, it circled her, belly low, tail whipping from side to side.

Instinctively Rachel crouched, placing her hands on the ground. She saw that her hands were caught in the indeterminate stage between man and beast, neither one thing nor the other. But she didn't know any way to speed up the change. She risked another quick glance towards the stables. Christine in her human form was still lying on the ground, clutching her shin.

Pain, Rachel realised. Pain prevents them from changing.

Camille hissed again, and Rachel saw the look of triumph in the panther's eyes. The cat spread her front paws and tensed her hind legs, ready to pounce. Then the creature relaxed, jaws gaping in an approximation of a grin.

She's playing with me! Rachel said to herself. Like a cat with a mouse!

Camille leaped. She landed just to Rachel's right, with her back arched and her fur standing straight up on her shoulders and spine. Rachel rolled to her left, and came up on her feet, running for the gate of the compound.

She had barely gone ten steps when the panther's weight thudded into her back, driving her to the ground. Rachel screamed as she hit the cobblestones, but she immediately rolled over and lashed out with her fists. She caught the panther a single blow across its nose and it pulled back, snarling viciously.

Rachel rose to a crouch. "See ... I can hurt you!" Rachel growled.

Camille hesitated. For a moment Rachel saw her begin to change back into her human form, her features flowing and distorted. But then Camille regained control and became a panther once again, ready to strike, to slash and tear.

When Rachel looked into the cat's eyes, she realised that Camille would show no mercy.

The game was over. There was no way she could win ...

She suddenly shuddered as a wave of nausea washed over her. She dropped to her hands and knees while her stomach churned ... and then the feeling passed and she felt the power flow into her. Rachel looked down at her hands again and saw that they were covered in hair, the nails twisting, hardening, turning black. The change was coming over her, but too slowly ...

Rachel snarled and leapt forward, landing on top of the panther, her jaws snapping, straining to reach Camille's neck. The panther roared, and tried to roll away, but Rachel was too strong, too fast. She locked her teeth on Camille's paw and bit deep, while tugging and pulling at the limb.

With a last reserve of strength, Camille lifted her back legs and drove them deep into Rachel's stomach, throwing her back. Rachel landed awkwardly on the stones, her foot turning beneath her. I'm dead, she thought.

But Camille didn't attack. Instead, she shrank back away from Rachel, hissing and snarling.

Caught in the half-stage between human and beast, Rachel staggered to her feet.

"No more."

Startled, both Rachel and Camille turned towards the voice. A huge bronze-skinned man was silhouetted against the evening sun. A large black raven perched on his shoulder. With the sun in her eyes, Rachel could not make out his features, but she could actually feel him watching her.

"No more," he said again. He gestured with his left hand and Rachel felt all the energy drain from her body. She was unconscious before she hit the ground.

12

STANDING IN THE DARKENED CARPARK, Madoc looked up towards the window of Rachel's hotel room. It was getting dark, so he was surprised to find that there was no light on in the room.

He wondered if Rachel was in the bathroom, or perhaps in another part of the hotel. But there was no way to be sure. He had no choice but to go up to the room and find out. Madoc didn't want anyone to see him in the hotel, so he would have to do it the hard way.

He checked that there was no-one around, then quickly removed his clothes and changed into his half-wolf state. He tied his clothes around his waist and began to climb.

Madoc had been a shapechanger all his life, and had almost complete control over his wolf-self. With a single thought he could transform himself into a huge, powerful wolf, or into something neither man nor beast, but with the advantages of both races: wolf strength and human dexterity.

He'd always thought that the one big disadvantage to being a shapechanger was the amount of clothes he went through. If something happened and he didn't have time to remove his clothes before he changed, they were invariably ruined. So Madoc always wore cheap jeans and shirts, and old sneakers without socks.

He moved swiftly up the face of the building, finding handholds with human fingers, gripping them with wolf's claws. He avoided the lighted windows and kept to the shadows as much as possible, though he knew there was little danger in anyone seeing him. Humans rarely looked up.

When he reached Rachel's window, he tapped gently on the glass. It was too dark inside for him to see anything but his own reflection, and it occurred to him that perhaps Rachel was asleep. He tapped harder but there was no response.

Madoc carefully examined the window. He bared his teeth in a grin; it was one of the new aluminium windowframes. Crouching on the window-ledge, Madoc hooked his claws underneath the aluminium frame, and tugged upwards. The whole lock gave way and the window swung open suddenly, catching Madoc off-balance, nearly toppling him to the ground below. He shrieked once, then he caught hold of the window-frame and pulled himself inside in one quick movement.

Madoc's night vision was excellent. Once his eyes adjusted to the darkness, he noted with alarm the devastation of the room. At least Rachel wasn't here. He allowed his body to flow back into its human form and dressed quickly as he examined the room in detail.

No wonder the window had opened so easily. The lock was already broken.

He breathed deeply, trying to ignore the cloying odours of spilled toiletries. Then he caught the distinctive smell of cats. Rachel's scent was there too, though it was very weak. She couldn't have been in the room for more than a few minutes. He sniffed again, observing that while Rachel's scent contained a certain amount of fear, she clearly hadn't been in the room when it was being torn apart. Her smell was newer.

Madoc looked around at the mess, wondering where she was now. From the evidence, he felt certain the cats had destroyed the room, then Rachel had returned, seen the damage, and gone looking for him.

He was about to shapechange again and leave the room the way he had come when he heard low voices outside the door. As he hesitated, the door was kicked open and two large security guards burst into the room. One of them flicked on the light. "Don't move!" he shouted at Madoc. "Stay right there!"

Madoc swallowed hard, knowing that they were sure to blame him for all the damage.

"What the hell do you think you're doing?" the older of the guards asked. "Jim, grab him!"

The younger guard nodded and swiftly caught Madoc's arms, pulling them around behind his back. "The police are on their way, kid! I don't know how you got in here, but ... " he stopped when he noticed the open window. "My God! You climbed in through the *window*?"

Madoc shrugged, trying to loosen the guard's grip. "No, I flew in. What do you think?"

"You're in trouble, boy," the older guard said. "The woman in the room next door said that she heard someone screaming. Where's the Ms Stone who's registered in here?"

"I was the one who screamed," Madoc explained. "I almost fell as I was climbing in. I'd like to find Rachel Stone myself, as a matter of fact. I was supposed to meet her here." He nodded towards the ruined bed. "I didn't do any of this, by the way. It was like this when I came in."

The guard called Jim replied. "Kid, you seem awfully calm for someone who's about to be charged with breaking and entering, and destruction of private property. Probably theft and assault as well."

Madoc smiled. "You can't keep me here. You might as well let go of me and save yourself a lot of trouble."

Jim pushed Madoc's arms up higher. "Are you threatening me?"

Madoc gritted his teeth. "No, I'm warning you. Let me go." Seemingly without effort, he jerked his arms out of the guard's grip. Then, before the man could react, Madoc swung around, grabbed him around the waist and flung him into the older man. Both guards crashed onto the wreck of the bed.

As Jim was getting to his feet, Madoc leapt up onto the window-ledge, pushed the window open, and jumped out.

The two guards rushed to the window. "No!" Trembling with shock, they leaned forward, looking for the smashed and bloodied body in the carpark below.

It was not there. The red-haired boy was nowhere to be seen.

Madoc's arms and legs were aching. It was definitely the highest he'd ever attempted to jump from, and changing into his half-wolf state in mid-air was something he'd never attempted before. If his timing had been off, he would have been killed.

As it was, the only fatalities were his clothes. They'd split at the seams and were more or less useless now. He felt it would be unwise to be caught roaming the streets of Dublin stark naked, so he changed into his full-wolf form. He wasn't able to move at more than a slow jog, but he knew he'd soon heal.

He padded out through the car park and into the street, keeping to the shadows where he could. He made his way back to the RDS, climbed over the fence and retrieved a spare set of clothes he'd stashed in some bushes, for just such an emergency. Then he allowed his flesh to flow back to its human shape, groaning aloud as human muscles protested. When he was dressed he made his way through the grounds to the stables, hoping against hope that he'd find Rachel there, waiting for him. He caught the faintest whiff of her perfume as he approached and his heart leapt.

Then he caught the odour of cat.

Stepping into the cobbled yard, he stopped to read the smells on the wind. Rachel had been here. And two other girls, both cat-people. They had fought and all of them had been injured; blood had been spilled.

But there was another scent. Madoc threw his head back, breathing deeply. It was a human odour, a male ... no, a shapechanger in human form. And the man had left behind a sense of incredible power; it reminded him of the odour that had clung to Piers de Courtney, the head of the Clan of Natalis. But this was stronger, far stronger.

And evil; old, cold evil.

13

THE NIGHTMARE SLID INTO DREAM, and the dream fragmented into reality.

Rachel woke with a throbbing headache and a sick stomach to find herself moving, swaying slightly backwards and forwards. She was aware of a great pressure on her stomach, and thought at first that something heavy had been placed there to prevent her from escaping.

As her head began to clear, she realised that she was tied to the back of a large hairy animal. She was lying face down, her hands and feet bound together, with thick leather straps securing her to the beast's body. Occasionally, her fingertips and toes touched the ground, scraping them raw. It was almost completely dark, but, by straining her neck from side to side, Rachel saw that ahead and behind flickering lights bobbed gently up and down. Torches, she realised.

The ground passing beneath her was unpaved, and there were hedges and trees on all sides. She could smell honeysuckle and herbs, dried grass and mossy earth. There were no city odours, no scents of people, so she guessed that she was in the countryside. Listening carefully, she thought she could detect the quiet murmur of voices, but couldn't make out anything specific, and couldn't even see the speakers.

Rachel turned her attention to the beast she was tied to. It appeared to be a large bear, or something very similar, but she knew there were no bears in Ireland. Its pelt was long and ragged, and badly in need of a wash – Rachel could feel its filth on the skin of her arms and legs, while the stench from the animal was over-powering.

She tried to piece together what had happened, but all she could remember was the figure of the huge man who had stepped between herself and Camille. Had he spoken? She wasn't sure. Had she fainted? She seemed to remember him gesturing, then the energy flowing out of her body, her wolf shape dissolving ...

She was no longer a wolf, she had changed back – or had been changed. Well, it was time to become a wolf again so she could escape!

Rachel concentrated, trying to remember how she had changed when she was fighting Camille. She vis-ualised her hands altering, her spine twisting, the bones lengthening ... but nothing happened. She tugged at the ropes tying her wrists, but they were too strong for her to break.

As she struggled, grunting with effort, someone ahead took notice and walked back. Rachel saw bare white legs and tiny feet and raised her head to look into the eyes of a pale-faced girl who couldn't have been more than eight or nine years old. She smiled at Rachel, showing a mouthful of ragged teeth. "You'll never break free, wolfgirl."

Rachel grunted. "Who are you?"

"The others call me Silky," the child replied, "because of my hair." She shook her head vigorously to reveal a mass of fine, snow-white hair. As Silky fell into step beside whatever animal was carrying her, Rachel got a good look at the girl. She was incredibly thin, wearing only a short, ragged tunic and strips of leather bound over her feet. Her eyes were clear, with pupils a peculiar shade of pale pink. Like the beast carrying Rachel, the pink-eyed child stank.

"You're not a cat," said Rachel. "What are you?"

Silky pursed her lips and scowled. "It's none of your business, wolfgirl. You're not in a good position to ask questions."

"Well," Rachel said, "there's not much else I can do. Let me guess, then. You're a slug?"

The girl snarled. "Be careful what you say, wolfgirl. There are a lot more of us here than you might think."

"I don't doubt it," Rachel retorted. "The smell is terrible. Does no-one in your clan ever wash?" she added with a cough. "So what *are* you, then? A rabbit?"

Silky looked away. "There is a great and powerful history to my clan," she said in annoyance.

Rachel knew then that she had hit the truth. "A were-rabbit, or were-hare. What next I wonder – were-mice? Where are we going?" she asked suddenly, trying to catch the girl off-guard.

"Home," Silky said icily, and slipped away.

Rachel twisted her neck to try and get a look at the others in the party. Now that her eyes had grown more accustomed to the dark, she was able to make out their shapes in the gloom. At the head of the column, silhouetted by the light of a flaming torch, was the large man

Rachel had seen earlier. The raven was still perched on his shoulder. Behind him, walking in a straggling group, were dozens of other figures.

Only some were human.

There was one who appeared to be half-man, half-fox. A tiny boy had the head and wings of a hawk, there were three or four rabbit-creatures like Silky, two tall women who changed into badgers as Rachel watched and a man with the curling horns of a stag growing from his head. The two cat-girls were close to the rear of the column.

Were-creatures, Rachel thought with a shiver. Not just wolves, but foxes, cats, rabbits ... a whole clan of were-folk. But what did they want with her? She looked again towards the figure at the head of the column. The answer, she knew, lay with him.

14

MADOC ABANDONED HIS CLOTHES and his human form again, and used his wolf-self's powerful sense of smell to track the people who had abducted Rachel. The cat scent was very strong in the compound in front of the stables, as was the smell of ancient evil from the clan leader.

Sniffing his way along the ground, he traced the scent to an area behind the stables, where it inexplicably vanished. Puzzled, Madoc tried to pick up the smell of the cat girls, but it appeared that they had been all over the area, and the trail was muddled.

Without being aware of it, Madoc whined softly. He knew that it was all his fault, that he should have insisted on staying with Rachel. At the very least, he told himself, he should have warned her that others were coming. Then she would have been prepared. Returning to the stables, he began searching once more.

The young police officer listened to the security guards' stories, and dutifully wrote them down in his notebook. He snapped the book shut and tucked it into his breast pocket. "Well then, sir," he said to the older of the guards, "You'd better wait around for the inspector to arrive. I'm sure he'll want to hear your story himself. Has anything in here been touched?"

The man looked around the wrecked hotel room,

and shrugged. "Not by us, but maybe by the lad who was in here."

The policeman did his best to conceal a sceptical smile. "This would be the same boy who jumped out the window and miraculously vanished?"

"I don't care if you believe me," Jim said, "but it's true. How else would he have got away?"

"Out the door, perhaps?"

Jim scowled. "If that was the case, why would I lie?"

"I'm not saying you're lying, sir. Now, please, just wait here until the inspector arrives, and don't touch anything. What was the name of the girl who was staying here?"

"Rachel Stone."

The policeman took out his book again, and jotted down the name. "S-T-O-N-E. Okay. And do you know where she is now?"

"No idea. She left the hotel in the late afternoon and hasn't been back."

"So you don't think she was here when the room was destroyed?"

"I doubt it. I mean, she would have said something."

"Unless she did it herself?" the police officer suggested. "She's not with a rock band, is she?"

The two security officers looked blankly at the policeman.

"Just a thought," he sighed.

At that moment the door opened and a well-built, middle-aged man entered. He showed his ID card to the police officer. "Detective Inspector Michael

Feeney," he said. He looked around at the mess, nudged some of the debris with his foot, then turned to the security guards and shook his head sadly. "I hear you had the lad and he got away."

"He jumped," the younger guard said, beginning to feel foolish.

"Do you know who the girl is?" The inspector's voice was gruff, obviously in no humour for playing games. "No, I don't expect you do. Her father is Robert Stone, a very influential man in the United States. And, I might add, a close personal friend of the Minister for Justice. She was staying here as an invited guest of the Dublin Horse Show and some big American association. I don't suppose anyone has bothered to check with the RDS?"

The three men shook their heads.

"Okay," growled the inspector. "Get on the blower. She may have gone to the RDS. I want three cars there in the next five minutes. Search the whole area. Work street by street, investigate the local restaurants in case she's out having dinner. Our first job is to find the girl ... then we'll sort out this mess. If there's no sign of the girl in the next couple of hours, we'd better inform her parents. And keep this quiet, understood? If the American Embassy gets wind of it, there could be an international incident."

The young policeman looked around. "You reckon it's a kidnapping, Inspector?"

Feeney uttered a short, harsh laugh. "A kidnapping! Let's hope not, eh?" Looking at the devastated room, he remembered the last time he'd seen a room in this condition, some months ago in Seasonstown House. He recalled the stories his men had told of the creatures that looked like wolves, but walked like men, and had attacked them as they guarded the house.

It could be nothing more than coincidence, but Inspector Michael Feeney didn't believe in coincidence.

There was no doubt in Madoc's mind: Rachel had been taken captive by other shapechangers. He'd traced Rachel's scent to the wall on Anglesea Road, then across the road and down the bank to the River Dodder. There the scent had disappeared. He'd scouted the opposite bank but found nothing. This meant, he believed, that the girl had been taken away on some sort of boat.

Still in his wolf-state, he returned to the RDS to collect his belongings: two spare sets of clothes, some food, a first-aid kit, and the little bit of spare cash he'd put aside for emergencies.

When he'd changed and dressed, Madoc took a last look through the stables. He patted Rob gently, and whispered some of the words he knew to calm horses.

Then he noticed something, just at the edge of his hearing: a low whining sound, getting louder, coming closer. Without thinking, Madoc rushed from the stable and across the compound, and swung his bag up onto his shoulder as he ran, seeking the source of the keening sound.

Suddenly the area was bathed in bright white light.

Madoc found himself surrounded by policemen.

"Don't move!" someone shouted, his voice distorted by a loudhailer. "Stay right there! Drop your bag and place your hands on your head!"

Madoc looked around frantically. The sirens had died down, but the lights from the police cars were still flashing, and the searchlights and torches burned into his eyes. Moving slowly, he pulled his bag from his shoulder and lowered it to the ground, then kicked it a few feet away.

The officer using the loudhailer stepped out from behind a car. "Now, very carefully, walk towards this car. Hands on your head, and don't make any sudden moves."

Madoc put his hands on his head and walked slowly forward, wondering how he could get past them all. When he reached the car, two policemen grabbed him from behind and cuffed his arms behind his back. "What's your name, and what are you doing here?" the man with the loudhailer asked.

"My name's Madoc Alton. I was only looking for a place to kip for the night. I didn't mean any harm!"

"He's just a kid!" one of the officers said.

The man with the loudhailer glared at him. "Shut up. Now, Mister Alton, tell me what you were really doing here. The truth, mind. If you lie, I can consider it resisting arrest."

Madoc looked at his feet, and said nothing.

"Get Detective Inspector Feeney on the radio," the senior officer snapped. "He's at the hotel." He turned back to Madoc and smiled. "This lad fits the description of the boy found in the girl's room."

Feeney! Madoc thought. He remembered the stout red-faced man from Seasonstown House last October. The policeman had been convinced that Rachel had been causing the damage to the place as a way of drawing attention to herself. However, by now Feeney must at least suspect the truth. Madoc knew that once Feeney got hold of him, there would be no escape.

The radio crackled and the three officers turned towards it, momentarily taking their eyes off the boy. He changed his hands, turning them beastlike from the wrist down. The handcuffs slid off. By the time they hit the ground, Madoc had vanished.

In his half-human, half-wolf state, Madoc could run for hours. He'd never understood where the energy came from, he just accepted it, as he'd always accepted that he was different from others. He liked being a wolf-man: the sheer speed and strength were almost addictive, and Madoc always felt puny and ordinary when he returned to his human form. When he took on his half-wolf shape, and especially his full-wolf shape, he felt alive, truly alive.

Now, he was running along the banks of the river, heading inland, hoping that he would pick up Rachel's scent once more. There were times when he wasn't sure whether the odour of cat and were-beast he scented on the air was real or imaginary. His only hope lay in the fact that the scents were heading towards the west ... and the rumours, the vague rumours of other were-folk always came from the west of Ireland.

Piers de Courtney, Madoc's clan leader, had always dismissed the possibility of other Clan Allta, however. He would point out that he had lived for hundreds of years and never encountered them. No-one had risked his anger by suggesting that perhaps these other were-folk didn't want to be found. Piers de Courtney had always been arrogant and proud; it came from the knowledge that he was stronger, faster than any human and capable of exercising the oldest form of natural magic: shapechanging. In time his arrogance had turned him bitter and evil.

Madoc recalled the scent of the strange man at the RDS. He too had left behind the same sense of old evil, of corrupt power. But he was obviously confident enough to travel, whereas de Courtney never ventured far beyond his den.

What did the stranger want with Rachel Stone?

Perhaps they didn't realise that Rachel Stone was more than Madoc's friend: she was another of the wolf-kind, the last of the Clan of Natalis. And he had made her a beast. That made her very precious to Madoc. More precious than he ever dared to dream.

The hotel car park pulsed with cold blue lights from dozens of police cars. Lengths of yellow plastic tape were strung around various areas, separating the sections which had already been checked from those that had not yet been scrutinised by the police. Officers were scouring the area, conducting a finger-tip search for clues.

From the manager's office, Detective Inspector Michael Feeney could see his men working as he was speaking on the phone to Robert and Elizabeth Stone. It was a difficult conversation. "No, sir," the inspector was saying, "No, I'm sorry, we have no idea, but I don't think it's a kidnapping."

"What leads you to that conclusion?" Robert Stone snapped.

"No ransom demand," the inspector said immediately. "I'm really just making this call to keep you informed of events here. I don't wish to alarm you unnecessarily."

"Well, you've alarmed us all right."

"What are you doing to find her?" Elizabeth Stone said, coming close to the phone. Her voice was choked with tears.

Feeney sighed. "To be honest, Mrs Stone, there's very little we can do at the moment. However, we are investigating all the local restaurants. It's my guess that Rachel is out with some friends. She probably doesn't even know about the room yet."

"Damn it!" exploded Robert Stone, "it's past eleven at night over there! Rachel wouldn't stay out that late. She knows better than that."

"Mister Stone, *please*. We don't know if anything's wrong. The only reason I called you is because of what happened in Seasonstown House last year. I simply wanted to reassure you that everything is under control at this end. There won't be any foul-ups like last year."

"I should hope not!" Robert said icily. "We're leaving for the airport now. We'll be in on the first available flight. I expect you to have some results by then."

The inspector made a face at the phone. "Yes *sir!*" Feeney slammed the receiver down so hard the plastic body cracked.

15

RACHEL WOKE SUDDENLY WITH NO INTERMEDIATE stage of dozing. She simply came fully awake, eyes wide.

Remaining still and unmoving, she tried to take in her surroundings. She was still bound hand and foot, and was lying with her back against cold stone in what appeared to be a large cavern. Enormous stalactites hung from the ceiling, while stalagmites jutted upwards like gnarled fingers. Judging from their size, the cavern was ancient.

Torches fixed to the walls at irregular intervals cast a butter-yellow light across the floor, deepening the shadows. Small groups of men and beasts – and creatures that were neither one nor the other – huddled around small bonfires throughout the cavern, murmuring quietly amongst themselves. The shadows they cast on the walls were monstrous. The stench in the cavern was appalling – a noxious combination of unwashed human flesh and dirty animal pelts mingled with dung and urine.

Rachel heaved herself into a sitting position, scraping her back against the stone. "Hey?" she called.

A dreadful silence spread around the huge cavern as hundreds of eyes turned to look at her. Then the eyes blinked out and the watchers dipped their heads as a huge figure strode across the cavern towards Rachel.

It was the man who had appeared at the RDS.

Rachel tried to back away, but the wall dug into her

spine. The shadowy form stopped in front of her, hands on his hips, then glanced over his shoulder and snapped his fingers. A young boy hurried forward carrying a torch, which he set into a holder in the wall above Rachel's head. Warm yellow light flowed over the man.

She had never seen anyone like him. He was easily two metres tall, extremely broad across the shoulders, and his skin was a deep bronze that seemed almost metallic. His hair was night-black, flowing in loose waves around his shoulders, but held off his forehead with a leather thong. His features were harshly handsome, with piercing blue eyes and a strong nose. He was wearing a simple knee-length tunic of rough grey cloth belted around the waist by a thick leather strap which was tied rather than buckled. The tunic was open at the neck, so Rachel could see that the man's well-developed chest was quite hairless. So were his arms and legs. Flat-soled sandals covered his feet, held on by thin leather straps rising around his calves to just below his knee.

The costume was almost primitive, but the face was keen and intelligent.

When the man crouched down and reached towards Rachel, she instinctively jerked her head away. With a slight smile, the man reached for her again, cupping her face in his huge hand. His hand was warm as he turned her face from side to side, studying it closely. His teeth flashed in a quick smile that accentuated his good looks.

"Who are you?" Rachel demanded to know.

Lifting Rachel's hands, he used his thumbnail to slice easily through the ropes that bound her. "I am Derg Corra Ua Diagre," he replied in a resonant voice.

The words were unfamiliar to Rachel. "Is that Gaelic? What does it mean?"

"Never mind. Just call me Derg, if it's easier."

"What do you want with me?"

"You are the wolf," he said simply.

"So?"

"I am the raven."

"What does that mean?" Rachel asked.

"When the wolf lies down with the raven, the shapechangers will be powerful once again."

She was puzzled. "Is that a quote? I've never heard it before."

"Of course not. Rachel, you have a lot to learn about the shapechangers, the Clan Allta." He sat down facing her, legs crossed, elbows resting on his knees. "You were bitten by Madoc, of the Clan of Natalis, on the night when the full moon appeared on All Hallows Eve. Thus he passed his curse on to you.

"But to us," Derg swept his arm around at the assembled individuals, "shapechanging is not a curse. It is a blessing, a gift we grant only to those we love. The Clan of Natalis did not see it that way, however."

"It happened by accident," replied Rachel. "Madoc bit into me as he rescued me."

"And you bitterly regret what he did," Derg said. "But you only see the curse, you do not see the blessing." He smiled, showing his perfect teeth again. "Look at me, Rachel. How old do you think I am?"

She studied his handsome face. "I don't know. You look about thirty, but I suspect you're going to tell me that you're a lot older."

He nodded. "I am over a thousand years old. No-one here numbers less than a hundred human years."

"Why do some of them look like children?"

"For many it is easier to wear the form from which they first ... changed. But shapechangers," he said simply, "can assume any form ... an ability you will soon master."

"Any form at all?"

He flashed his charming smile again. "Well, within certain parameters. You, for example, are essentially a werewolf, which makes it easiest for you to take the form of a wolf, although in time you might try other ... experiments. Eventually you will discover that you can control your *human* form as well. You have already experienced a hint of this power; soon, I promise you, you will be able to call upon your wolf strength or wolf speed while remaining fully human."

Rachel bit her lip, then asked, "What do you want with me?"

Derg tilted his head to the side and regarded her thoughtfully. "You will find that out later. But I assure you, Rachel, you will come to no harm." He took her hand in his. "You have my promise on that. In fact, you will be treated as you never have been before."

Looking around, Rachel saw that the others were still staring at her. "Where did all these people come from? I thought that the Clan of Natalis was the only group of shapechangers left."

"That's what *they* thought, too. But the Clan of Natalis were too arrogant, too proud. I would not even consider allowing them to join with us. A long time ago there were thousands of shapechangers. The legends of every race and people tell of us. But the humans hated and feared us. When they turned against us, they hunted us down like the beasts that we were ... while forgetting that we were also humans. A thousand years ago, I gathered together the last of the Clan Allta, the shapechangers, in Ireland. I brought them to this place. Here we have lived, hidden from human eyes, safe for the moment."

"But you said that when the wolf and the raven lie down together, the shapechangers will be powerful again. You intend to make yourselves known again?"

"When we are strong enough. Not yet, though. It will take some time." Derg's eyes suddenly blazed with cold blue fire. "I have long dreamt of the day that I would lead my people out of the darkness of these caves and back into the world. A thousand years ago, I swore I would find a land for my people. I will keep that promise. All we want is somewhere to live in peace. Can you imagine what it's like to be shunned by normal society, to be hated, dismissed as a fiction, a nightmare monster? No, you can't truly understand that, you still think of yourself as human."

Derg's words chilled her. "You're saying that I'm *not* human?"

"You are one of us, now. Part human, certainly, but much more than that."

"Tell me, Derg, is there any way to remove the curse?"

He leaned forward and rubbed his chin. "I've told you this is not a curse. Why would you wish to throw away such a blessing? Knowing what you know, why would you wish to return to your original human form? It seems so fragile, so short-lived and vulnerable."

"I didn't ask for this," Rachel told him bluntly. "And I don't want it. Several times, I have come close to killing people."

"But you didn't. You're not a killer at heart, Rachel. None of us are, believe me. We do what we must to survive, like any species. That's all."

"What about Camille and Christine? They would have killed me!"

Derg glanced over at one of the small groups. Cats and humans stared back. "They made a mistake. I merely asked them to find you and see if you were as powerful as I sensed. They were not supposed to hurt you."

"And am I? As powerful as you thought, I mean?"

"No. You are much more powerful. I am aware of this, though I don't know the reason for it. Perhaps it is simply an inborn gift. But I assure you – when you realise the full strength of your powers, Rachel, you will never want to be human again. *Never!*"

Derg flashed a smile he obviously meant to be

charming. But there was something cold and calculating beneath his good looks; something that lurked behind his smiling eyes and sent a sudden chill up Rachel's spine.

16

MADOC HAD BEEN RUNNING FOR almost eighteen hours before he was finally forced to stop and rest. In that time he had picked up and lost Rachel's scent seven times, and he had come to the conclusion that the trail had been deliberately obscured. The further west he travelled, however, the stronger the scent became. He had been able to distinguish some other animal odours as well: cat, fox, dog, rabbit, deer, badger, even a pig.

Now, resting at the side of a clear stream, in the shade of a giant oak tree, he changed back to his human form. Then he washed himself in the stream and dressed. With his aching feet dangling in the icy water, he ate the last of his food, some stale sandwiches and half a gnarled apple.

He knew that he had been seen several times during the day – the screams of people were evidence enough – but he didn't care, and who was going to believe their stories of a huge wolf-man loping across the country?

Time was running out. He had to find Rachel as soon as possible. In two days the moon would be full again, and he'd have little control over his wolf-self. In the half-madness that came with the total change, he might forget the importance of finding the girl. By the time he regained his senses, it could be too late.

If only he knew why they had taken her ...

It was dark when Madoc awoke.

Animal senses brought him fully alert. He'd slept for most of the afternoon, exhausted by his run. His body was stiff and aching now. Pulling off his clothes, he stuffed them into a bag and allowed the change to alter his body – partially, but not completely. While still retaining his basic human shape, he took on a wolfish appearance. Lengthening muscles and a sudden increase in his metabolism banished his aches and pains. Throwing back his head, he breathed in the evening air, searching for traces of Rachel.

Instead he found a number of humans. Ten or twelve men close by. Scared. Angry. Madoc could also detect a faint odour of cordite: the men were carrying rifles and shotguns.

They could be hunters or poachers, but Madoc wasn't waiting to find out. He turned and ran in the opposite direction, following the flow of the stream, using his animal strength to carry him away from the men with guns. He ran swiftly, not caring if they heard him, relying on his speed to outdistance danger. They spotted him soon enough, and, shouting, gave chase.

But why didn't they fire? he wondered.

Perhaps they were afraid of hitting someone ahead of him!

Even as he was changing direction, the wolf-man's foot snagged on a taut, fine wire, which looped itself around his flesh, biting deeply. He fell hard. Suddenly the forest was ablaze with lights and sirens.

"We've got something!" a man's voice called.

"Marker twenty-three, down by the bank!"

Madoc gazed around in panic, but he was dazzled by the lights that had been fixed high in the trees. He worked frantically at the wire entrapping him while dozens of people streamed through the trees towards him.

He heard them whisper 'wolf-man' and 'wild boy' and suddenly realised that perhaps too many people had see him racing along the lonely country roads and across the fields.

The men gasped when they realised what they were seeing. Many of them blessed themselves and backed away, though none lowered their guns.

"Holy God! What *is* that thing?" someone asked.

One man shook his head in bewilderment. "This isn't real. No way! It's just someone dressed in a costume," he insisted, pointing with his shotgun and trying to sound confident.

"Okay then," said another man. "*You* go and take his mask off. Where do you want your body shipped?"

A large, hard-eyed police officer stepped forward. "All right, lads, that's enough." He stared at Madoc for a few seconds, then turned to one of his colleagues. "Get on to the station, Bill. Tell them we've got a situation here. Get on to the zoo, too. Tell them it's not an escaped wolf, it's ... " He looked at Madoc again. He wasn't sure what it was. He turned to the men around him. "Any of you others even *think* about leaving, and you'll be spending the rest of the night in a cell. If word of this gets out we are going to have a nasty situation on our hands. Half of Ireland will be in a panic, thinking the devil's after them, and the other half will be mobbing us, wanting to see this thing and get souvenirs."

The reports had been coming in to police stations for the past day and a half: a wolf, a dog, a hairy man, a wild man, a bear, had been seen racing across fields. As the various reports were compared, it was discovered that sightings were following a roughly straight line from Dublin, heading south-west. A dozen traps had been laid along the creature's route, though no-one had honestly expected to capture anything. Especially not a wolf-man.

But now they had him. And they hardly knew what to do with him.

Sitting on the ground, Madoc turned his head slowly, staring at each of the men in turn, wondering how he was going to escape. He could complete the change, become a total wolf, and try and dart away during the brief interval of surprise. But they would surely shoot, surprised or not. Or he could change back into his human form, but they might be frightened enough to shoot him anyway. In the end, he realised that the only thing that was keeping them from killing him was the fact that he was something they had never seen before.

He finally loosened the knot of twisted wire around his ankle. It had cut deeply into his flesh, and his skin was sticky with blood. The wind picked up. He lifted his head and sniffed. For a single instant, he caught the faintest trace of Rachel's scent. Fading away ...

He knew then that he must act at once or lose her entirely. As he got slowly to his feet, he discovered a large rock half-buried in the ground.

Guns shifted to follow his every movement.

Slowly, deliberately, Madoc cleared a patch of earth with his foot. With the tip of a nail, he began tracing intricate symbols in the dirt.

"What's he doing?"

"Maybe he's trying to communicate."

Madoc stepped back and, while the men leaned forward to examine the shapes he had drawn in the dirt, he swiftly bent and seized the rock. In one smooth movement he hurled it at the nearest bank of lights.

The light shattered in a tremendous explosion of sparks. The hunters instinctively ducked. One discharged his gun into the ground, almost blowing off his foot.

Madoc whirled and charged through the startled group, knocking the men aside. One stepped in front of him and raised his rifle, but Madoc reached out and yanked the rifle from his grasp and sent it spinning into the river.

By the time the others had regained their composure, Madoc was long gone.

17

SHE THOUGHT SHE'D SPENT A DAY – perhaps two – in the cavern, but it was difficult to judge time in the perpetual gloom. She knew it was a long time, though, because more than once the burnt-out torches had been replaced, and there had been five meal breaks – raw vegetables and boiled fish.

She hadn't seen Derg since her first encounter, and the only restriction that had been put on her was that she was not to attempt to escape. Breege, a deer-woman who had been assigned to watch over her, pointed out that the cavern was at the centre of a warren of caves. "Unless you know the tracks and turns you would be hopelessly lost very soon," she warned Rachel. "And you wouldn't want to be lost in here. Some of the lower caves are haunted by the ghosts of Clan Allta."

The walls of the cavern were covered in finely drawn pictograms and tiny images. Some were in perfect condition, but many of the lower ones were battered and broken. She was standing by one panel running her fingers over the broken stone trying to feel the picture, when Breege appeared, carrying two wooden bowls of greasy stew.

"Do you know what these pictures mean?" Rachel asked her.

"They show the history of the Clan Allta in Erin," the tiny, big-eyed woman replied. "But that's all I know.

Only Derg can tell you the full history of the shapechangers."

Rachel closed her eyes and ate the stew. She found it helped if she didn't have to look at it. "Does no-one ever leave here?" she wondered.

"We all leave here at some time or another. Derg allows us out for brief periods. It's hard," Breege added, "especially at the full of the moon when the change comes over us. But we know it's for our own good. We must be prepared, must know what it's like ... outside." Her voice began to vibrate with passion. "When Derg leads the shapechangers back out into the world, we'll never have to skulk in caves again!

"Every year more and more of us are allowed out to stay. There's a badger couple living in County Kerry. They have a small farm where they live as normal humans; they even have friends in the local village. During the time of the full moon, of course, they keep very much to themselves. Then they roam the woods in their badger form."

"Has no one discovered what they really are?" Rachel wanted to know. She had lived among humans as a werewolf, so had Madoc and his sister. How many such creatures were walking undetected among humans?

"They're leading a normal, happy life," Breege assured her.

"So why don't the rest of you do that?"

Breege sighed. "It's an experiment that Derg organised, to see if they can fit in with human society.

Unfortunately, it took a lot of time to set up. After all, officially none of us even exist, so simply arranging a place to live is very difficult. To get money, Derg trades some of the few treasures he tells us he has amassed over the years just for this purpose. But there's not many of them left, not enough to set us all up in places of our own."

"How long has the experiment been going on?"

"I don't know. As long as I can remember," the deer-woman replied. "Derg gets annoyed if we ask him about it too often. He says that every time it looks like everything's all right, technology marches on another few steps and everything has to be redone. It's the human farmers, you see. They keep putting up barbed-wire fences and traps. Some of them even have electric fences now. If the badger couple was snared in a trap and their secret discovered, then people would start hunting for us. It would be ..." She fell silent for a few moments, then gave Rachel a brave smile. "But things are going to improve soon, Derg says." The smile slipped a little and a desperate yearning showed through. "They must! It's terrible to live like this, in a den underground ... "

Rachel nodded soberly. "I should think so. But if Derg says things are going to get better ... it's something to do with me, isn't it?"

"I'm not allowed to say." Breege stood up abruptly. "I should get on with my work, I suppose."

The girl watched the young woman pick her way across the cave and crouch by the spring that bubbled up on the far side, supplying a constant source of fresh water. Rachel was idly wondering if the spring was fed by some underground stream that led outside, when a shadow fell across her. Even before she looked up, she knew it was Derg.

"You have the look of someone who is plotting escape," he accused.

Rachel felt her cheeks burn with guilt. "Do you read minds too?"

Derg laughed and sat down beside her, his back resting against the wall. "No, but if I was in your position, I would be thinking of running away too. I should apologise for kidnapping you, Rachel. But I didn't think you'd join us willingly, am I right?"

"Yes. Please, you have to tell me what you want me for."

Derg's raven flapped down from a perch high on the cave wall, and landed on its master's shoulder. Tilting its head, the bird regarded Rachel with hot yellow eyes.

"I want you – I *need* you," Derg began. He stopped and took a deep breath. "I need you to save the shapechangers!"

Rachel looked at him blankly.

Derg waved a hand, encompassing the entire cavern. "The clan trust me. They are convinced I can save them from this living death, they *know* that I can bring them to a new life in the world outside. I haven't the heart to tell them that I cannot. I am powerful, the most power-ful shapechanger alive today, perhaps. But I cannot save them alone. I need your help," he added earnestly.

Derg continued, no longer looking at her but speaking almost to himself, "I was born a shapechanger in a time when the Clan Allta walked this world unafraid. I was part of Fionn Mac Cumhaill's Fianna. The name probably means nothing to you, girl, but once we were the finest fighting force in the world. The legends of Arthur the Briton and his knights are but shadows of the stories of Fionn and the Fianna.

"I was proud then, arrogant. In time I even came to consider myself greater than Fionn. I challenged him for the leadership of the Fianna. I thought that with my shapechanger strength and speed, I could defeat him. But I was wrong.

"Fionn cast me out of the Fianna, and for a while I lived as a bandit in the wild forests that covered much of Erin in those days. Gradually, I gathered together an army of Clan Allta. I was determined that once I had enough allies to defeat Fionn, I would march on Tara and wrest it from Conor Mac Airt, the High King." Derg smiled bitterly. "I told you I was arrogant – and I overestimated my own abilities. My army was defeated, humiliated. Then Fionn called upon his ancient powers to banish us from the land, 'never to walk in the sun, nor breathe the noonday air, nor habit with mortal men, until the raven lies down with the wolf on the sand.'

"He bound us under a *geas* – an ancient binding spell – and thus we have lived these many centuries. And of course, because there were no wolves left in Ireland – except for the werewolves – the prophecy was not

100

fulfilled. We would not attack other were-folk – not then. But we always feared that someday we might be driven to it. When the Clan of Natalis was destroyed, however, I thought we were truly doomed ... until I discovered you."

"But you can walk in the world above," Rachel protested. "I've seen you – you and the others."

"Only for a short time," Derg replied. "Then the sun hurts our skin, and the light makes us uncomfortable. We are truly children of the night."

"But what about the badger couple living in Kerry?" the girl asked.

"They only survived three moons," Derg said softly. "I've never told anyone. I allow the others to think they still live and are happy, so as to give them heart." He turned his face to Rachel, his eyes brimming with moisture. "So now you know. You are the chosen one," Derg said, staring deep into her eyes. "You are the wolf; I am the raven. Together, we can break this ancient spell."

Rachel started to shake her head, but Derg ignored her.

"Tomorrow night," he went on, "when the moon is full and we are at our strongest, you and I will take on our beast forms and fulfil the ancient prophecy. The wolf will lie down with the raven. Then my people can go free."

"What do I have to do?" she asked nervously.

"An ancient Brehon ceremony, similar to that of marriage."

"Marriage!"

Derg bared his teeth in a smile. "It has no significance, I am not saying we will really be husband and wife. It is simply a ritual necessary to break the spell."

"Suppose I refuse to do this?"

"Then you are condemning these people to spend the rest of their lives in this cavern. And remember, their lives are much longer than a human's."

"That's emotional blackmail," protested Rachel.

Derg replied, "I agree, but what choice do I have? I am the raven, you are the wolf. It might be hundreds of years, if ever, before another wolf appears in Ireland."

"You're not giving me much choice, are you?" Rachel whispered.

18

THE TAXI SCREECHED TO A STOP outside Rachel's hotel. Robert Stone threw a handful of money at the driver and jumped out. He dashed across the car park and into the lobby, where he found Detective Inspector Feeney waiting for him.

"That was quick," Feeney said, stretching out his hand. "Broke a few speed limits on the way from the airport, did you?"

Stone ignored the gesture. "Where's my daughter?"

The inspector ran his hand across the back of his head, smoothing down his already perfect hair. "I don't know," he admitted. "There's been no sign of her since she left the hotel. We've gone through her room and although there is plenty of damage, nothing is missing, neither items of clothing nor personal effects." He handed Stone an envelope. "We found her passport and these traveller's cheques untouched. So I think it's safe to say that she didn't run away."

"No kidnap demands?"

"None."

"So what are you doing? Where are you looking?"

"Mister Stone, we're looking everywhere. Literally. To start with, we checked every hospital and doctor's surgery, in case Rachel was in an accident or something. Then we started checking the hotels, hostels, guest houses, campsites. The ports and airports are under observation. As time goes on, we're widening the search area. We've also been in touch with New Scotland Yard and asked them to look out for a girl travelling alone." He put up his hand to stop Stone's flood of protests. "I know, it's not likely that she'll go to England, but we have to consider the possibility."

Robert Stone took a deep breath. Since the call from the police inspector he felt as if he'd been living in a nightmare. "You said that her hotel room had been totalled!"

Feeney nodded. "Right. Come with me." He led the American to the elevator, and while they were waiting for the lift to descend to them from an upper floor, he asked, "I thought Mrs Stone was coming with you?"

"Elizabeth stayed behind at the airport, to collect the baggage and organise a hired car and arrange hotel accommodation for us. She'll probably be here in a couple of hours."

"And you left her out there by herself? Mister Stone, if this *is* a kidnapping – "

The lift pinged and both men stepped inside.

Robert Stone shook his head. "She's not alone. I hired two private bodyguards before we left Los Angeles."

The inspector was about to remind Stone that the carrying of firearms was illegal in Ireland when the elevator stopped and the doors opened. "Rachel's room is along here."

The two uniformed officers standing outside the room snapped to attention as the inspector approached. He nodded curtly to them as he pushed open the door and allowed Robert Stone to precede him into the devastated bedroom. "The room's very much as we found it. We've dusted for prints, and taken samples of everything. I've had forensics working on this almost round the clock."

"So what have they found?" Robert whispered, looking around in horror.

Feeney walked over to the window and stared out. "Aside from my own officers, the two security guards, the girl who does this room, and Rachel herself, there have been three people here. At least according to the hair samples. We've got fingerprints from all of them; they appear to belong to two young females and a young male. The boy we already know about, though we have reason to believe that he's not directly involved. I'll go into that later." The inspector paused and took a large breath. "However, that's not all we found. We did discover evidence that there had been two – how can I put it? – two large cats in the room."

Stone frowned. "Cats? Rachel hates cats," he said absently.

"More specifically, panthers, Mister Stone. One of the lab assistants couldn't figure out some of the hair samples, and decided – purely on a whim, he said – to try a broad-spectrum search. In plain terms, they didn't know what the hair was, so they looked it up in the computer. The hairs belonged to panthers, two separate animals. I know it sounds crazy, but it's for real. We brought in an expert on large cats from Dublin Zoo, and he was able to match the scratches on the walls with the claws of a panther."

Robert Stone swallowed. "Panthers. But ... Oh my God! Do you think that Rachel was ... I mean ... "

"No," the inspector said firmly. "No. Rachel wasn't here when this happened, and there were no traces of blood, or anything to indicate that she was hurt."

"But I didn't think panthers were native to Ireland ..."

"They're not. There are no big cats in Ireland."

Robert sat down in a chair from which half the stuffing had been torn. "This is crazy," he muttered.

"And it doesn't get any easier. Now this you're *not* going to believe. Have a look out this window beside you. See how high up we are? Well, the boy the hotel security caught in the room apparently climbed in this way. Not only that, this is how he escaped, too. He jumped out. From six floors up."

"Did he survive? You make it sound as if he landed on his feet and walked away."

"That's what it looks like," Feeney admitted ruefully.

"There was no body?"

"None."

Stone gazed out the window in silence for a few seconds, then said very softly, "I read in the newspaper that there's a wild beast roaming the countryside. One of the papers claims all the police are out hunting a wolf-man."

Feeney looked uncomfortable. "Insane, isn't it? We've got a hunt underway all right, but it's for your daughter, Mister Stone. I don't know where the papers get their ideas from."

Robert Stone turned from the window and folded his arms across his chest. "You were at Seasonstown House, Feeney. You know what happened there; your own men reported seeing wolf-men. You think this is somehow connected to that?"

The inspector regarded him coldly. "No, I don't. My men saw large dogs. That's what it says in the reports."

Robert gestured around the wrecked room. "You saw Rachel's room in Seasonstown House. It looked just like this."

The inspector shrugged. "Attempted burglaries can get pretty rough. Maybe that's all we have here."

The other man snorted derisively. "The boy who was found in this room, what colour hair did he have?"

"Red," Inspector Feeney said.

"The boy who pulled Rachel out of the burning house had red hair."

19

THE SCENT WAS WEAK, TWO DAYS OLD at least but strong enough for Madoc to be certain. Rachel and her captors had passed this way.

The boy was close to exhaustion. He had travelled hundreds of miles and, following his encounter with the hunters, had been forced to travel mainly by night, keeping his human form during the daytime. The trail had cut right across Ireland and ended on the outskirts of the Burren, an eerie and desolate limestone 'moonscape' in County Clare, on the west coast.

Changing to his full-wolf form, Madoc began sniffing frantically along the ground, trying to establish the direction of the trail. Loping along on all fours was much more practical then travelling on two human legs. Time was running out; it was now late afternoon, and the full moon would be rising in less than five hours.

He sniffed among the great slabs of stone and the clumps of wild vegetation, eliminating the odours of strange flowers and herbs, the saltiness that permeated the air, the limestone tang of the rocks. When he finally managed to locate Rachel's trail, he dashed back, grabbed his bag in his mouth, and set off running.

The scent grew stronger, fresher, leading him deeper into the strange Burren wilderness. He followed it into the heart of the Burren, twisting and turning over the ancient cracked rocks, taking care not to catch a paw in the fissures. A broken paw would be disastrous now.

The trail finally led him to a hollow in the midst of a particularly inhospitable stretch of landscape. It was close enough to the sea for him to smell the salt, and the rocks were speckled with white seagull droppings. Crouching on the lip of the hollow, he breathed deeply. The scent of Rachel was strong here ... but it was overlaid by the odours of a multitude of beasts.

He had found her. His tail thumped the ground, and he had to resist the temptation to throw back his head and howl his delight. I've found her. I've found her!

Finding her was only half the problem. Rescuing her was going to be far more difficult. He was exhausted now; he knew there was nothing he could do until he had rested. Slithering backwards on his belly, he discovered a clump of rocks jutting upwards like the fingers of a hand, and he slid into the centre. It was cool and dry inside, and he could watch the cave entrance without being seen.

Lying flat on the stony ground, he rested his head on his paws, trying to ignore the rumbling in his stomach, the aching in his limbs. His eyes closed slowly. He jerked them open and sat up, not willing to fall asleep, not now, not when everything was so close.

Then he lifted his head with a start, realising that he *had* fallen asleep, though judging by the position of the sun, he knew it had only been for a few minutes. He was trying to remember what had awakened him when he heard a slight rasping on the stones.

Madoc pricked up his ears and swivelled his head to

follow the sound. He sniffed quietly, and thought he could detect the scent of cats. His half-exhausted mind took too long to reach the conclusion that if he could smell the cat ... then it could smell him.

Madoc turned his huge head. He was too slow – the sleek black panther was already in mid-air, razor-sharp claws extended, gleaming fangs bared.

Instinctively Madoc twisted away, avoiding the full weight of the panther. But he did not move fast enough to escape its slashing claws. Fire blossomed across the back of his neck, though his heavy pelt prevented the panther's claws from tearing deeper.

Howling, Madoc rolled onto his back, knocking the panther's claw free. Then he dodged aside as the cat's snapping jaws barely missed tearing out his throat.

There was no way he could defeat the panther. Not now; he was exhausted, and hadn't eaten or slept properly in days. The cat crouched, hissing like boiling water. Its jaws worked, forming words. "You losssst, wolfman. Lossst. Girl is ourssss."

Then the cat leaped.

20

MADOC DROPPED TO HIS BELLY ... and the panther sailed over his back, claws slashing the air where his neck had been only a moment before. The big cat hit the ground hard and tumbled over. Before it could get to its feet, Madoc leaped onto its back, sank his teeth into its neck, and began tearing, ripping, shaking the cat from side to side.

The panther roared in pain and anger and tried to dislodge the wolf, but Madoc clung on grimly.

And then without warning, the panther began to change, its form twisting and changing beneath him. Madoc instinctively jumped clear. He found himself staring at a dark-haired young girl, the same age as Rachel. Blood was streaming from the wounds in her neck and sides as she lay unmoving on the ground.

He sniffed cautiously, nudging her head with his muzzle, but she didn't react. She was still breathing, however. Already the wounds in her sides were healing. Then as Madoc leaned over the girl, her fist came up in a solid blow that caught him full on his sensitive nose. Red and yellow stars danced before his eyes. The shock sent him flickering into his human form.

When he looked back to the girl, he discovered that she was gone.

Madoc searched until he found a speckled trail of blood leading away. He realised that she hadn't been as badly wounded as he'd thought; perhaps she had only pretended. Now she would be able to warn the others. He had to stop her.

He charged down the small hill, following the trail of blood. At the last moment he glimpsed a huge shape crouching in some bracken. He tried to stop but the scree shifted beneath his feet, causing him to lose his balance. He had no time to recover before the panther was on him again.

She struck Madoc in the chest, sending him crashing heavily to the ground. He locked his hands around the panther's neck, trying to keep her teeth away from his throat, but even in her weakened state she was far too strong for his human form. The snarling jaws pressed closer to his throat while the cat's front claws tore ragged scratches in his shoulders.

Madoc suddenly relaxed his grip for a second. The panther, who had been putting all her effort into getting at his throat, crashed head-first to the ground. The boy pushed her dazed body away from him, then ran with all his might. Rocks and loose shale slithered treacherously beneath his feet, but this time he managed to keep his balance. Risking a quick glance over his shoulder, Madoc saw that the panther was getting up.

With a last burst of energy, Madoc initiated the change. He got as far as the half-wolf, half-man form – and kept running.

Somewhere, he told himself, I've got to find a place to hide. If I don't, I'm dead!

21

RACHEL STOOD UP AS BREEGE, the deer-woman, approached. The tiny woman was struggling beneath the weight of a long, apple-green dress she was carrying across both arms. Stopping in front of the girl, she bowed deeply. "This will be your wedding gown. I hope it fits."

The words disturbed Rachel. To disguise her embarrassment she lifted the dress off Breege's thin arms and examined it closely. It was made of layer upon layer of heavy silk, sewn with the most exquisite workmanship. The high neck, lace collar and broad cuffs were ornamented with thousands of tiny seed pearls.

"It's beautiful," Rachel whispered, impressed in spite of herself. "I've never seen anything like it."

"It's from the fifteenth century," Breege told her. "Derg said that only the best is good enough for his bride."

Rachel bit her lip. "I haven't said yes, yet." She was trying to remain calm. Giving in to fear would not help her now, she knew. But her heart was pounding so violently she thought surely the deer-woman could hear it.

"You must marry Derg, Rachel." As Breege spoke, her huge eyes brimmed with tears. "You must, for all our sakes. Just think of it, Rachel. In a few hours this curse can be lifted and we can be *free*! Can you imagine what that will be like for us? How much it means to people who have been condemned to darkness for so long?"

Rachel handed the dress back. "No, I don't suppose I can. How much time is left?"

"Another hour, then we have to begin preparations. We'll come for you when everything's ready. And we are so grateful to you!" Breege could not resist adding.

Hiding in the shadows, Derg watched as Rachel and Breege discussed the wedding. He nodded with satisfaction. Everything was going according to plan. Obviously the girl suspected nothing. He turned to leave, though he left his raven to watch over Rachel. The bird could act as his eyes and ears.

He threaded his way through a maze of tunnels to his own private chamber deep in the heart of the earth. None of the other shapechangers visited this small room, and none knew of the network of tunnels that lay beyond it.

Derg's chamber was small and bare, and contained only the minimum essentials: a blanket of straw for a bed, a small bowl for food, a single torch in a holder, and a large tapestry on the wall, its pattern faded over the centuries to a muted blur. The room was crudely hewn and badly lit, with deep pools of shadow. Derg had lived in this depressing chamber for more than a thousand years ... but today was the last day.

He pulled the tapestry to one side, revealing a low entrance to a series of secret tunnels. Stooping to avoid hitting his head, he stepped through the entrance and allowed the tapestry to fall back behind him. A few faint pinpoints of light percolated through the worn fabric, but as soon as Derg moved away from the opening he was plunged into darkness.

The big man made his way forward confidently, his fingers trailing along the wall. He turned left and left again, finally emerging in an another vast underground cavern. The walls and ceiling were coated with a luminous green moss that shed an eerie glow. This was Derg's personal storeroom. It was littered with the accumulation of a dozen lifetimes: cloaks, swords, spears, statuettes and standards, chests spilling jewels, pots disgorging thousands of gleaming coins. Incongruously, piled against one corner were modern items like rucksacks, water bottles and tents, binoculars, cameras ... items that he had stolen from the people he'd met throughout his long life, or from travellers who had ventured too close to the cavern's entrance-way in the Burren above.

At the centre of the cavern was a large circular pool of still water. The shimmering fungal light reflected emerald on the water.

Derg picked up a small gnarled stick, crouched in front of the pool, and stirred it slowly in an anticlockwise direction. Widdershins, they had called this action when he was young. He concentrated on Rachel, and then watched as her face appeared in the water. Every day for the past thousand years the same face had gazed up at him from the pool. Those eyes, that haughty expression, had imprinted themselves on his memory until he was convinced they were bound up with his own destiny. Such loveliness, such innocence, such ...

Such a shame she has to die, he thought. Then he chuckled.

22

MADOC'S LIMBS WERE TREMBLING WITH EXHAUSTION, but still the cat pursued him. He knew that he could have outrun the beast in the first few moments when she was dazed, but then she would have been free to get a warning to the others of her kind. So he had decided to lead her out into the Burren, trap her somewhere, then double back and find Rachel and her captors himself, without having to fight off the panther.

The sun had finally set. Madoc had less than an hour before the full moon rose.

In his half-wolf state, his night vision was excellent. He could see the panther at a distance, sniffing around the base of a huge rock. He had already circled the rock twice, making certain to leave his scent, then climbed the boulder and jumped as far away from it as possible. He hoped that it would take the panther a long time to realise she had been tricked again.

He snatched a few moments' breather, then jumped to his feet, deliberately sending a rock tumbling, making as much noise as possible, bringing the beast to him. Then he ran. The panther lifted its head, saw him, and gave chase, its snarls echoing flatly across the limestone landscape.

A large cluster of rocks directly ahead caught Madoc's attention. The formation didn't look natural, though it appeared to have been in place for centuries. The boulders were large and flat, two huge slabs laid horizontally across four others, forming a crude box.

If Madoc could lure the panther into the box, he might be able to trap her there.

He caught the edge of the nearest slab and hauled himself up onto it. His teeth flashed in a grim smile. Once he got the cat inside the box, he could wall up the opening.

The wolf-man glanced over his shoulder. The panther was moving straight for him, bounding easily over the uneven ground. He had less than half a minute to prepare ...

Madoc braced his legs against the ground and heaved. The slab shifted an inch. He pushed again, the stone rubbing his shoulders raw. The tongue lolled from his mouth and he was panting with the effort.

The slab suddenly shifted and slid aside with a rasping, grating sound, revealing a deep pit beneath. A well? A mineshaft? Far below, what looked like a tiny silver coin sparkled in the dull light.

Cat!

He was turning as the snarling panther crashed into him, knocking him backwards. He caught hold of the cat as he swayed on the edge of the pit, but the weight of the big animal was too much. Before he had a chance to howl his terror he fell, still clutching his enemy.

"I wish there was a mirror here somewhere," Rachel said, "so I could at least see what I look like." In spite of her growing anxiety, she could not resist the magic of the dress, the exquisite green dress. Wearing it, she could – for a moment – almost believe she really was a bride about to marry a man she loved.

But in reality, something terrible was happening – or about to happen. With every moment that passed, she was more convinced of it.

"Trust me," Breege said. "You look beautiful."

Silky, the rabbit-girl, nodded agreement. "We're all so proud of you. In the years to come, we will set aside this day as one of celebration. Your name will become part of the Clan Allta folklore, the beautiful stranger in a silken gown."

Rachel looked ruefully down at the lustrous fabric. "Remember that tonight's the full moon. This gown won't last long when I go through the were-change."

"But the timing is vital," Breege explained. "Derg said that the ceremony must take place in the last few seconds before you change."

"What will happen then?"

"I don't really know. No-one does."

Rachel took a deep breath. Her heart was pounding again and her mouth was dry. It was all too vague, no-one would tell her anything. She had a sense of walking into gathering shadows. But she was determined not to panic; that never helped. Keep calm; try to think. She lifted her chin and said, "All right. I'm ready now."

A raven flapped into the tiny cave that had been set aside for Rachel's use. It perched on Silky's shoulder and tilted its head to look at the American girl.

Moments later, Derg appeared in the cave's entrance. "You look beautiful," he said, with what sounded like sincere admiration.

"Thank you," Rachel replied stiffly.

Derg was wearing a long, hooded robe, tied at the waist with a white rope. A twisting Celtic broach was pinned high on his left shoulder. In his right hand he carried a long wooden staff topped with a ram's horn. He was still handsome, but there seemed almost a *dark* brilliance about him that made Rachel want to keep her distance.

"This is not how I'd imagined my wedding day would be," she admitted. "Will we really be ... *married*?"

With another of his dazzling smiles, Derg stepped forward and took her hand. "This is a genuine Brehon ceremony," he explained, "but our marriage will be in name only: the symbolic marriage of raven and wolf. The ritual which is necessary to negate the ancient spell contains several parts, and this is an important one. Once it is complete, you can return to your own world ... if you wish. Or you could stay and I would train you in my ... arts," he added, watching her carefully.

"I would like that," Rachel said, but she was lying and suspected he knew it. She was trying to be brave, but her lips were trembling. She felt as if the world were narrowing down around her, squeezing her into a small corner. There was no way to escape, she had no choice but to submit. Yet her horror mounted with every moment. The idea of being married, in any way, to the master shapechanger was increasingly terrifying. No one particular thing frightened her. Her fear was the sum total of his expression, his words, and the very atmosphere around him.

Run, she told her legs. *Run.*

But they could not. They were trembling too much.

Derg looked around at the other shapechangers. "Now. We are ready." He reached out and seized Rachel's hand and led her into the main cavern.

An enormous cheer rang out, howls, clicks, screeches and hisses echoing off the walls. Derg smiled. "Every shapechanger in the country is here today to witness this."

Not everyone, thought Rachel. Madoc isn't here.

"Now, the ceremony!" gloated Derg. "It begins here among our friends, and will end just as the full moon rises, when we are strongest, when the beast that lives in man – and in every woman – comes to the surface."

Rachel nodded. "What do I have to do?" she asked in a tiny voice.

The ritual seemed simple enough. First Rachel and Derg stood facing all those present and proclaimed themselves members of the ancient order of shapechangers. They further swore that what they were about to do was not for themselves, but for all shapechangers. Derg made some strange signs in the air while a female were-bear crushed some bitter herbs that released a pungent perfume into the chamber.

Then one by one, creatures of myth and legend came and bowed before the couple, vowing obedience and presenting gifts. Someone began singing at the back of the cavern, an eeric, thrilling melody to the accompaniment of a set of small bagpipes.

Foxes, dogs, cats, badgers, bears, rabbits, hares, even squirrels paraded up and down, their feet following some ancient pattern that was not quite a dance. Music, if it could be called that, rose and fell until the cavern's echoes made Rachel's head ache unbearably. And still the ceremony continued; still more of the clan appeared and had to be presented.

Rachel felt herself sagging as time dragged by. She glanced sidelong at Derg and realised that he too looked tired. She wondered how long it was until the moon rose. Surely it was soon.

She turned to Derg to ask him, and stopped, shocked. Derg was more than merely tired. He looked ... *old*. Even as she watched, he raised his hand – the strong, straight fingers suddenly gnarled with age, the veins exceedingly prominent – and pulled his hood over his head, covering most of his face. But she had already glimpsed the deep lines appearing around his eyes and mouth. The skin was sagging beneath his chin and he seemed to be smaller than before. No, she corrected herself, he was *stooping*, like a very old man. And now he wasn't just holding the staff, he was leaning on it. As she watched he inched back into the shadows. He doesn't want them to see, Rachel thought.

With a mighty effort, she kept a smile fixed to her face. She didn't need her animal instincts to know that something was terribly wrong. She knew Derg was more than a thousand years old, but he had always looked so youthful, so powerful.

She looked around at the other shapechangers. They smiled back at her, their happiness genuine. They believe everything he's told them, Rachel thought. They don't even question him. They think that they're going to be saved tonight as a result of this ritual marriage and all the trappings that go with it.

But what if none of it were true?

The thought struck her like a blow.

Derg was a liar by his own admission. He had lied to every shapechanger here tonight about the badger folk in Kerry. So, how much of what he had told her was true? Could she believe any of it?

But she must pretend she did. She had to play their game – until she could find a way to escape.

If there was any way to escape.

Derg glanced over at her. "Are you feeling all right?" he asked. His once-strong voice was thin and reedy with age.

Rachel turned towards him, noticing with disgust that a long string of saliva hung from his wet, cracked lips. "I'm fine," she said, doing her best to keep her voice calm. "I'm just a bit nervous, that's all."

"There's no need. Everything will be perfect, you'll see." His voice wheezed into a rasping cough. "Forgive me. The full moon takes its toll, you understand."

Rachel looked to Breege, but the deer-woman didn't seem to notice that anything was wrong. She smiled at Rachel with tears of happiness in her huge brown eyes.

"Long life and happiness to you both," she murmured.

What if I'm wrong? Rachel thought suddenly. What if he *has* been telling the truth? If I get out of here somehow without going through with this ritual, I would be condemning these people to live in this cavern for the rest of their lives.

Derg reached out and took her arm with his aged, wrinkled hand. "It is almost time, Rachel. Come with me." He raised his voice and for an instant the old strength flowed into it and it boomed across the cavern. "You must *all* come! There is a place in these caves that you do not know about, a place that has been waiting for a thousand years for the marriage between the raven and the wolf!" His hand trembled; his long ragged fingernails bit deeply into Rachel's arm. She hadn't the strength to pull away.

As he regained consciousness, Madoc groaned aloud. He ached all over. The last thing he could remember was falling, still struggling with the panther ...

He sat up and looked around. The broken body of the panther lay a few feet away from him, at the edge of a pool of clear water. He crawled to her and turned her over. He could tell she wasn't dead. Members of the Clan Allta returned to their human forms if violent death overtook them in spite of their natural longevity. But she had broken several bones and lost a lot of blood. He ran his hand across her broken front leg, feeling the muscles shifting and twisting beneath the skin as the damage repaired itself. She was young and healthy, and tonight was the night of the full moon, when her powers would be at their strongest. By morning she would be whole again.

Madoc then gazed around with growing astonishment at their surroundings. They seemed to be in a huge cavern littered with valuable loot. When he looked up, he could see stars through a hole in the cavern's ceiling. That's where we fell in, he thought.

He could see something else, too. A changing light in the night sky that told him he had only minutes before the full moon rose. His every instinct warned him to get to Rachel before then. He breathed deeply, drawing in the smells of the place, trying to see if he could pick up Rachel's scent, but she hadn't been in this cave. However, it was full of the distinctive evil odour of the master shapechanger.

This must be his lair, Madoc thought. This is where he works his evil.

On the far side of the cavern was a dark hole that proved to be an opening. When he warily passed through, Madoc discovered a vast network of tunnels beyond. Much would depend on the choice he made now. A false turn could leave him wandering, lost in the tunnels. Many of the tunnels smelled stale, disused. One, however, was strongly tainted with the odour of the master shapechanger. Madoc followed it cautiously, hands stretched in front of him, head ducked low.

Light appeared. Shadows danced on the stone walls.

Voices. Coming closer. And ... a familiar scent. Rachel was nearby! And voices were approaching – many voices.

Madoc turned and ran back along the tunnel to the cavern with the pool. There he hastily concealed himself and the wounded panther beneath a pile of fabric.

"Through here," instructed Derg in his cracked and ancient voice. "Into my private quarters."

Some of the shapechangers exchanged glances. They had never been invited into their leader's chamber before.

"There are too many of us, master," Breege said. "The room won't hold us all."

Derg chuckled. "Nonsense!" He strode across the small chamber and ripped the tapestry from the wall, revealing a tunnel entrance beyond. He turned to smile at Rachel, who saw with horror that his teeth were now hanging loose in his receding gums. "Please forgive me for being so weak on our wedding night, my pretty one. It is a combination of excitement and the moon. It will pass soon, I promise you."

Someone handed him a torch. Derg carried it into the tunnel, pulling Rachel after him. In spite of his weakness he still had enough power in one hand to grip her arm so tightly she could not hope to get away. "You are nervous, Rachel?" he inquired as he felt the tension in her arm. "You shouldn't be. I may seem repulsive to you now, but I trust that you have the ability to see through mere physical appearance, and appreciate the person beneath."

Rachel bit her lip and said nothing. Her instincts were warning her to flee. They were the same instincts that had kept the wolf alive through centuries of persecution, the subtle hints and clues that warned of danger. Had she the power, she would have willingly assumed her wolf form right now and fought to escape with fang and claw.

Derg's bony fingers tightened still more on her arm. It felt almost as if he was holding onto her for support.

Eventually they reached the immense cavern with the pool. Derg shuffled up to the water, then stood peering down into it as he waited for the other Clan Allta to join him.

Entering Derg's storehouse for the first time, they gazed in wonder at the piles of gold coins, the swords and spears, the bales of cloth, luxuries such as they had never seen before. But it was to the pool that their master called their attention. "This is the Pool of Knowledge and Power," he explained to them. "In less than a minute the full moon will clear the horizon and we will begin to change. We are strongest then." He smiled; a hideous smile of shrunken gums and rotten yellow teeth. "We are truly the children of the moon." His voice broke into a cackling, mirthless laugh.

Behind Rachel the shapechangers were beginning to move about uneasily, sensing that something was wrong.

"Is this part of the ceremony?" Rachel asked.

127

"Oh yes," Derg hissed. "This pool is a sacred place, ancient beyond reckoning. The gods themselves bathed in its waters. It is said they created the myriad races of men and beasts from this pool."

Everyone was staring at Derg now. His hood had fallen back and he was swaying to and fro, eyes wild and mad as his voice rose into hysteria.

"There are men and there are beasts ... and there are the Clan Allta, the shapechangers. Men have always placed us below them, but in truth we are greater than men. We are the step between humans and gods. But there is an ancient legend, first told by the shapechangers who came out of the Land of the Nile, that this pool in the land at the edge of the world can make shapechangers into gods!"

Rachel tried to back away from Derg, but the other shapechangers were crowding too closely. She could feel the hairs on the back of her neck rising up, and it wasn't just because she was afraid. The change was beginning.

"The pool must be prepared, you understand," Derg said, his ancient eyes glittering. His lips had drawn back over his teeth until his grin was purest evil.

Rachel swallowed hard. "How must it be prepared?" she asked, stalling for time. But time to do what?

Derg reached into his robe. "With blood. The blood of a very special being."

Rachel gasped when he withdrew his hand and she saw the gleaming knife he held. "It is silver, my dear," he told her. "Silver ... to kill a werewolf."

23

BURROWING BENEATH THE PILE OF ROBES AND BLANKETS, Madoc listened as best as he could. But he too was beginning to feel the first effects of the full moon. His head was buzzing, his limbs aching.

At his feet the unconscious panther stirred uneasily.

Madoc eased some of the robes aside and peered out. He saw the master shapechanger holding Rachel by the arm, his tight grip drawing blood where his fingernails bit into her skin. Rachel was beginning to change. She was swaying slightly, and her hair was noticeably growing as the bones of her face altered and became more prominent.

Madoc took a deep breath, shifted his position a little, and waited for the right moment. He watched with pounding heart as the old man raised the dagger to the girl's throat. Derg moved slowly, relishing Rachel's fright. The other shapechangers were increasingly nervous about the situation, but their own change was coming over them too.

Derg placed the sharp blade of the silver dagger against Rachel's skin ...

Now!

Roaring at the top of his voice, Madoc erupted from the huge pile of robes. In his excitement he did not notice the pool yawning at his feet until he pitched forward, losing his balance on its rim. He fell into the water with a mighty flailing of arms but was out again almost instantly, hurling himself towards the stunned old man. He threw all his weight against Derg, knocking the silver knife from his grasp.

Some of the quicker-thinking shapechangers tried to grab Madoc but he fought free of them, his strength enhanced by fear and rage.

He caught Rachel as her eyes rolled upwards in her head and she collapsed. Then, using his bulky, hard-muscled wolf shape, he shouldered his way through the other shapechangers, snapping and snarling at them as he ran from the room. Those at the back didn't know what was happening and simply stepped aside to allow him through.

"Stop them!" the old man shouted in a desperate voice. "Stop them!"

Madoc raced into the tunnel he had followed earlier. Rachel was growing heavier in his arms. He looked down to discover that it wasn't because he was getting tired: she actually *was* becoming heavier as she slowly turned into her half-wolf form.

Not now, Madoc pleaded silently. Just a few more minutes, please!

The tunnel led to Derg's small private chamber. In the entrance, Madoc paused to look back. Two large boar-men were charging towards him. Both had almost completed their change and were running on all fours, squealing savagely. Vicious tusks erupted from their gums, and their small, beady eyes held the red light of murder.

In Madoc's arms, Rachel moaned and twisted from

the pain of the change. He realised he could not carry her any farther, not until the transformation was over. He placed her down gently, then turned to try and keep the boars at bay and give her time.

The first stumbled as it reached him. He took advantage of the beast's clumsiness to lock his fists together and strike down as hard as he could, hitting the creature on the back of the head. The were-boar's forelegs buckled and it fell to the ground.

The second hesitated and blinked. Then it feigned an attack. Madoc twisted to one side in an attempt to avoid its charge, but the boar twisted too, and he felt a sudden, searing pain as one of its tusks raked along his ribcage. Meanwhile the first boar was getting to its feet. With a grunt of fury it charged, succeeding in pinning Madoc against the tunnel wall. Tusks scored his legs, his thighs, and opened gaping wounds along his arms. But this was the time of the full moon and the wounds were closing almost as soon as they opened.

Madoc knew, however, that it was only a matter of time before the other shapechangers caught up.

Suddenly a great dark shape came bounding up the tunnel. Enormous claws sank into the coarse hide of the boars attacking Madoc. The figure lifted them from the ground with apparent ease, cracked their skulls together with a sound like colliding boulders, then hurled the two bodies back down the tunnel into the midst of the other shapechangers, knocking down the leaders and effectively blocking the passageway.

Madoc gaped in astonishment as the newcomer

loomed before him, huge and terrifying, muscles rippling beneath a covering of coarse golden hair. The figure was vaguely human, but animal-like too. The form flickered and rippled and for an instant – a single heartbeat – a girl smiled from behind a wolf's mask.

"Rachel!"

"I knew you'd come to find me," she growled.

24

DERG LAY WRITHING ON THE GROUND, MOANING.

Over the past few centuries the change had been becoming more and more difficult for him. The ageing human tissues found it difficult to cope with the transformation into his beast shape. The change had never been this bad before, however. He could feel his joints expanding beneath his skin, his muscles straining and pulling, the bony plates in his face attempting to come together to form the bird's mask that was his changed form.

He had been so close ... so close.

The blood of a werewolf, the oldest form of the shapechangers, when spilled into the pool and then fired by the light of the full moon, would have made him into a god.

His eyesight was fluctuating, flickering between colour and shades of grey, between two and three dimensions. He stared at the pool. The moon was reflected like a silver coin dropped on dark green velvet.

So close. All the pool needed was blood.

"Blood ..." he muttered through clenched teeth " ... for the sacrifice."

From far off in the tunnels he could hear the roars and screams of Rachel and the other werewolf as they were torn apart by his loyal shapechangers. They thought they were doing what Derg would have wanted. Instead, they were destroying his last hope. I have failed, he said to himself. The pool needed pure blood, shapechanger blood. Rachel was so perfect, but now she was gone, her blood spilled and dirtied on the tunnel floor. Wasted ...

It had all been for nothing. And there would be trouble to follow. The other shapechangers had seen his treasures. When they could again think clearly, they would wonder why he had not told them about his wealth. Why he had not shared it with them. They would begin to suspect that he had lied to them ...

Once more the change twisted his body in agony, his limbs thrashing against the ground as he rolled onto his back. The muscles of his shoulders bunched together, forming tiny wings. Coarse black feathers sprouted from his skull, piercing through his skin like red-hot needles.

After a few terrible moments the pain eased. With a great effort, Derg pushed himself to his knees. He hadn't been able to assume his bird form completely for the last century and a half.

When he looked at the pool again, he saw that the shining water was swirling and turning as a ghostly vapour streamed upward, slowly evaporating into nothing.

A sudden moan startled him. He turned to see Camille come staggering out from beneath a pile of blankets and robes. The cat girl walked awkwardly, as though she had broken bones which had not healed properly. But she managed to stumble into Derg's arms, where she began purring like a huge kitten.

"Master, I'm so glad to see you. I did my best, but the wolf-boy beat me. Forgive me. Forgive ..."

Derg hugged the girl. "Aaah, Camille, always the most faithful of my followers. Dear, innocent, trusting Camille." He ran his talon-like fingers through her bedraggled fur, smoothening it.

The pool needed blood.

"It's all over now, Camille," he said sadly. "The wolves have won, I fear."

Just a little blood to fire the ancient magic. The blood of a shapechanger. The perfect, werewolf sacrifice was lost, but perhaps some lesser offering would at least partially accomplish what he wanted? There was no other choice. He must try ...

Derg's fingers stroked the cat's back, feeling the broken bones knit and join. Then he reached for the fallen dagger.

25

RACHEL RACED THROUGH THE TUNNELS, following the strongest scents.

Madoc ran close behind the girl, panting with the effort to keep up. He was stunned. He had never seen Rachel's half-wolf form, and he'd never imagined she would be so powerful. She was at least two feet taller than he, and broader across the shoulders. And she was fast, faster than Madoc at his best.

As they ran, Rachel explained why Derg had kidnapped her. "He told me he wanted to lift some ancient curse and free the Clan Allta. He lied. He wanted to sacrifice me in order to make him into something all-powerful."

"He's mad," Madoc replied. "A thousand years of life would make anyone mad."

They reached a dead end, and Rachel stopped abruptly. "Now what?"

Madoc shrugged. "I don't know. We'll try another tunnel. We don't want them to trap us here."

Rachel snarled. "Let them come! They can't stop us."

"They might not be able to stop you, but they'll certainly stop me. I've trailed you clear across Ireland. I haven't eaten or slept in two days. I've been attacked by panthers and gored by boars. You may be fit and healthy, but believe me, I'm not."

Rachel patted him on the shoulder as though he were a complaining child. "Don't worry, Madoc, I'll look after you."

A sudden thought struck him. "Rachel ... something's very wrong here."

She stared at him blankly.

"Something's happened, I tell you! There's a full moon out there and we aren't crazy! We should have lost our minds by now. We should have reverted to our beast state."

Rachel raised her hands and looked at them. Madoc was right. They should have transformed into paws. She should be running on all fours. "What does it mean? The others aren't effected, they've all become beasts."

"Then it must be something we've done ... something ... It's the pool," Madoc said suddenly, excitedly. "It has to be the pool. I fell into it, I was soaked through. When I carried you in my arms, the water from the pool must have got on you as well."

Rachel shook her head. "I don't see ..."

"It could be the cure," Madoc said simply.

Derg stood up from Camille's twitching body and watched as the girl's blood mingled with the milky water of the pool.

Camille wasn't dead: he'd stopped just short of killing her, and already her body was beginning the process of healing.

When the waters of the pool had completely changed colour, Derg dropped the silver knife on the ground and stepped into the pool. All he needed was a little strength ... just enough to go hunting the were-wolves.

They raced around the corner – straight into a group of shapechangers. Badgers, foxes, deer and rabbits scattered in confusion. The foxes were the only ones who posed any sort of threat, and though there were three of them, they were much smaller than Rachel and Madoc. One of the foxes bravely darted forward, snapping at the girl. Rachel picked it up and effortlessly tossed it into the group. She was about to attack the others when Madoc stopped her.

"No, Rachel! We have to get them to the pool, it's the only way to save them."

"Save them? Don't be a fool, Madoc. *They* are the ones attacking *us*!"

"But that's because they can't reason when the moon is full. Because the animal part takes over completely. If we can get them back to the pool, they'll become like us. Then we'll be able to reason with them."

"I hope you're right about this!"

Madoc nodded. "So do I. Let's see if we can lead them back to the pool. Once they've been through the water we can make them see how Derg has deceived them."

It took little effort for Rachel and Madoc to push through the milling crowd of shapechangers. They ran just fast enough so that the shapechangers wouldn't lose sight of them, but not so fast that they could catch up.

When Madoc glimpsed Derg's chamber before them, he relaxed slightly. "It's almost over," he told Rachel. "This will be the last time they go mad at the full moon."

"On the contrary, wolf-boy," came a voice from the room ahead, "nothing will change for them. For you, however, it *is* all over!"

A shape filled the doorway. Then a creature from a nightmare padded out into the tunnel as Madoc and Rachel backed away in horror.

From top of head to tip of tail, Derg was six metres long. His skin was green and scaly, reflecting the torchlight as it exuded an oily sweat. He crouched on four stubby feet that ended in razor-like claws. A long spiked tail flicked from side to side, rasping off the stones. The head was set into the body without a neck. The face was recognisably Derg's, except for the eyes, which were lidless, completely white except for black vertical slits. A forked tongue flickered on the air.

"Impressive, yes?" Derg asked Madoc. "This is just *one* of my forms. Once I was trapped in the form of a raven. But with age comes knowledge and with knowledge comes power. Now, I can be anything I want to be. It's been a long time, though, since I took on this *peist* shape." He turned to Rachel, tongue flickering wildly. "I was right about your great power, wolf-girl, but I was wrong to think that I had to have *your* blood for the pool. Your old friend

Camille proved sufficient." As they watched, Derg's form twisted and flowed into a huge panther.

Behind Rachel and Madoc, the other shapechangers arrived, stopping short when they saw the huge beast towering over them.

Then Derg changed back into a man, though taller and much more muscular than he had been before. "However," he said, "I still prefer this shape. It makes me a little more acceptable to the common man, don't you think?"

"Run!" Rachel cried to Madoc. "Get out of here, I'll hold him off as long as I can!"

"No way," replied Madoc, drawing himself up to his full height. "I'm staying with you."

Derg sneered. "Stay, run, it doesn't matter. You're both going to die anyway."

"What about the others?" Madoc asked.

"I don't need them any more. I don't think I ever did. They will die too. I will be the last shapechanger. And in this world of puny men, I will be a god."

"The rest of the Clan Allta might disagree with you," Rachel said calmly. "And they'll fight. They will do anything they can to stop you."

Derg lashed against the wall with his fist, cracking the solid stone, crumbling it to powder. "They are nothing! *I* am all-powerful!"

"I don't think so," said Rachel quietly. Madoc marvelled at how calm and composed the girl could be under such stress. All her strength was not on the outside. "You used Camille's blood to fire the pool," she went on. "That was a bad choice. She was weak, almost dead from her wounds, and she was evil. Evil weakens. I think that if you had used me, you *would* have been unstoppable. But not now."

Derg laughed, the sound bitter, filled with age-old hate. "Never fear. When I'm finished with you, I will feed your blood to the pool. Then I will be complete, omnipotent."

Behind Rachel, the other shapechangers scattered and ran. Derg took a step forward, his hands changing into razor-sharp claws, a thick, barbed tail appearing at the base of his spine, curling horns poking through his hair.

Rachel and Madoc glanced at each other, then turned and fled the hideous apparition.

It was useless. Derg caught up with them in a single leap, locking his powerful claws around their necks. "You pitiful fools. You can't fight me. You can't escape. All you can do is die!"

26

MADOC TWISTED HIS NECK, snapping and snarling at Derg's arms, but his teeth slid harmlessly off the man's scaly skin.

Swiftly, Madoc changed into his full-wolf form. The shock of the change loosened Derg's grip, and Madoc dropped to the ground. He scampered out of reach, then turned and ran.

"Hah! See that? Your fellow wolf deserts you, Rachel. He is even more of a coward than I thought."

"Let him go," Rachel demanded. "And put me down!"

"I will do no such thing. Do you take me for a fool? No, Rachel, you and I have work yet to do. But not here, not here," he muttered. "Somewhere safe, quiet. There we shall complete the ceremony."

"What ceremony?"

"The ceremony which ends in your death. I cannot allow you to live. You are not strong enough to stand against me now ... but in a century or two, who knows?"

Rachel's eyes flicked desperately from side to side as Derg carried her through seemingly endless corridors.

Madoc, where was Madoc? He wouldn't desert her, she knew that. Throwing back her head, the wolf howled her pain, but the sound was swallowed by Derg's laughter.

Madoc watched silently as Derg dragged Rachel past his hiding place. He waited until he was sure that he wouldn't be seen, then darted back along the corridor, and into Derg's room. He ran into the tunnel and made his way to the pool room, walking blindly along the narrow tunnel.

He was certain that Derg's power came from the pool, and it was his only hope.

He almost didn't see the small, crumpled cat lying at the edge of the pool. The pathetic bundle was quivering slightly, and Madoc thought she was close to death. He wrapped the little creature in one of the blankets, then dipped his fingertips into the water and brushed it against her lips.

The cat promptly opened her eyes. Her pupils dilated in fear when she saw him.

"Don't be afraid, I won't hurt you," Madoc said, as he tore up another of the blankets and used it to bandage her wounds. "I think you're going to be okay," he lied. "How do you feel?"

The creature coughed. Once she had been a huge and terrifying panther. Now she was diminished to this small shape, helpless in the arms of her enemy. "I ... think I'm dying," she whispered.

"No, you're not. You've lost a lot of blood and body mass, though. What did he do to you?"

"He ... he cut me! He wanted my blood to mix with the water in the pool."

Madoc looked at the pool, where the crimson-tinged water was evaporating at an abnormal rate. From the piles of Derg's treasure he selected a crystal bottle stoppered with a cork and filled it to the brim. A brief search located a leather thong which he tied around the neck of the bottle, so he could sling the container over his shoulder and carry it with him. Then he turned back to the injured were-cat.

"Listen to me," he told her. "Lie still, now. Is there anyone here who can help you?"

"I want Christine," she said weakly.

"Who is she? Where can I find her?"

"She's in the main chamber. Clan sister."

"Okay. I'll tell her you're here." Madoc stood up to leave, but turned back when he reached the entrance. "What's your name?"

"Camille. Yours?"

"Madoc."

"The sea!" Derg exclaimed thankfully, emerging from a Burren cave to stare out across the moonlit waters of Galway Bay. "We won't be disturbed here. The Clan Allta fear the sea, Rachel. They think the salt will kill them. Superstitious beasts."

The girl scornfully replied, "You're calling them superstitious! You were the one talking about a thousand-year-old curse."

"That's not superstition, it's simple truth. Today you humans accept as normal what your parents would have considered impossible." He barked a harsh laugh. "But look at me! There has never been anything like me

144

before. Never. *I* am the impossible. Stronger, faster, more powerful than any living human. Nothing can stand in my way. *Nothing* can hurt me!"

"You've been living in that cave for too long," Rachel told him. "A lot has changed in a thousand years. Science has made a lot of changes, hundreds of new ways to kill things."

Derg threw Rachel roughly to the sand. "Regain your strength. I want you to be fit ... before you die."

Rachel lay back on the sand, rubbing at her neck. She needed time to think, time to plan. She needed to keep him talking. "That pool – what is it? Madoc suspected that something in the pool prevented the beast form from taking us over."

Derg crouched down in front of her. "I would call the pool magic. Not everything can be accounted for by science. There are some things you have to take on faith. When the pool is fired with blood under the light of the full moon, it acquires special qualities. It can turn a shapechanger into a god."

"Could it reverse the process?" Rachel asked, "and turn a shapechanger into a human?"

"If the faith was strong enough."

"I suppose you'll try and keep me prisoner until tomorrow night," speculated Rachel, "then complete the ceremony. The moon will still be full then."

"No. Your wolfine friend ruined all that when he opened the hole in the cave's ceiling. The moonlight will sap the power from the pool, evaporate the water." Derg reached out and grabbed Rachel's arm, hauling

145

her to her feet. "I could have made you great, Rachel Stone," he said with what sounded like genuine regret.

Madoc followed Rachel's distinctive scent out through the tunnels. As he neared the exit, he encountered one of the were-boars. The creature lowered its head and charged him, but he dodged aside. He poured a tiny amount of water from the pool onto its back as it ran past him, however.

The change was startling. The creature's form flowed and altered, becoming recognisably human beneath its coarse bristles. "What happened?" it cried in a high-pitched squeal.

"No time to explain," Madoc replied. "Go back to the pool, and save as much of the water as you can. It's ... a cure. Then find your people and give them the water."

Without waiting for a reply, Madoc ran off through the tunnels in search of Rachel.

In his arrogance, Derg had made no attempt to disguise her scent. It led the wolf-boy through disused tunnels and across echoing caverns. All were empty, but some bore evidence of occupation in the distant past. Soon, Madoc caught the distinct smell of sea air. A few moments more and purple light studded with stars appeared ahead. The tunnel opened out onto a stony ledge. Waves lapped, hissing, just below.

Rachel screamed.

As Madoc burst from the tunnel, Derg hurled her into the water.

27

MADOC LEAPT ONTO THE MASTER shapechanger, driving him to his knees.

Derg swiftly rolled up onto his feet, already transforming himself into a raging beast with the body of a rhinoceros and the fangs and forearms of a lion. He ran at Madoc, but his great weight made him slow. Madoc leaped nimbly over the monster's back, then darted out of reach.

Rachel rose spluttering from the sea, her wolf pelt plastered against her skin. She was growling deep in her throat. While the beast was turning around for another charge, she waded out of the water and ran to Madoc's side.

"Split up!" Madoc cried to her as the beast lumbered towards them. "He can't come after us both!"

They ran in opposite directions, parallel to the shore, but Derg ignored Madoc and concentrated on Rachel. The master shapechanger flickered into a black panther, a leopard, a mountain lion, as he attempted to catch her. The girl had slipped into her full-wolf form, a creature normally able to run faster and longer than the big cats who pursued her. But the rocky beach was treacherous underfoot. She was not able to reach her top speed. With the help of his magic, Derg was gaining on her at every bound.

Rachel rounded an outcropping of stone and suddenly found herself trapped in a tiny cove. To the left was the sea, to the right and directly in front, sheer cliffs. Derg was behind her. Rachel flickered back into her half-wolf form and leaped as high as she could, claws digging into the cliff face as she began pulling herself up. The cliff was wet and slippery, and the claw-holds few, but Rachel wasn't going to give up. Where there was nothing to grip, she pounded at the rock until it splintered and cracked, then forced her claws into the cracks.

Far below, Derg watched, laughing. "You'll never make it, Rachel. If you fall from that height, not even you will be able to survive."

Ignoring him, the wolf-girl climbed higher.

Then, slowly, Derg realised that Rachel *was* going to make it to the top of the cliff. And once she was there, she could run for miles.

He pondered for a second, examining the cliff, trying to think of a form that could climb it with ease. But why climb?

He concentrated. The bones of his skull began to shift once more, his nose and upper jaw elongating into a beak. It had been a long time since he had been able to take the form of the raven completely. But now he was stronger than he had ever been.

When Rachel next looked down, Derg was nowhere to be seen. With a sigh of relief, she continued climbing, though slower this time, taking more time with her hand- and foot-holds.

After what seemed a lifetime, she finally reached the top. She hauled herself over the edge and rolled onto her back, her breath coming in great heaving gasps. Her nails were torn and ragged and the skin on her hands and forearms was rubbed raw. She knew they would heal shortly, but right now they *stung*. When she'd caught her breath, she turned over, crawled to the edge and looked down again. Derg was still missing, but far along the beach she could see Madoc running towards her.

She frowned. Madoc was waving his arms and shouting, but his voice was swallowed by the wind and waves. Wolf instinct saved her. She turned as the huge raven swooped down on her, claws and beak extended.

Rachel screamed and lashed out frantically, but the raven kept its distance. Its face changed slightly, until it resembled Derg once again.

"You are beaten!" he cawed triumphantly. "I can change into anything I wish. There's no way for you to escape!"

Rachel pushed herself to her knees and glared defiantly at him. "Come on, then! I'm tired of running, I'm tired of being chased. Fight me!"

Derg screeched again and prepared himself for another attack. "As you wish!"

Madoc thought that his lungs were going to burst from the effort, but he wouldn't let himself stop. Ahead, Rachel and the giant raven were tearing at one another. But the wolf was no match for the savage bird, and Madoc could see that Rachel was losing, being driven back towards the cliff edge.

He put on another spurt of speed, but he knew he was going to be too late.

As he watched, the raven swooped low and came rushing at Rachel with incredible speed. It collided with her, and Madoc saw Rachel stumble. The cliff gave way beneath her feet, toppling the girl backwards.

Over the edge.

28

AS SHE FELL, RACHEL INSTINCTIVELY reached out to save herself. She grabbed Derg's talons, hoping the were-raven would have enough power in its wings to hold her up.

It didn't.

Rachel and Derg plummeted over the edge of the cliff together, crashing onto the rocks far below.

Tears brimmed in Madoc's eyes and he cursed himself for being too slow. A small part of his mind told him that at least Derg Corra Ua Diagra was finished, at least his thousand-year reign of evil was over. But it was little consolation.

He stumbled blindly forward, splashed through the shallows and climbed onto the jagged rocks to get at the bodies. Derg was still alive, but only just. He was constantly changing, fading from one form to another, becoming man and beast and creatures that were neither. But Madoc ignored him to get to Rachel. He was startled to see that she was still in her half-wolf form, which meant that she was still alive, though only her remarkable power was sustaining her.

When he touched her she opened her eyes, staring unseeingly past him. Lifting one hand, she tried to touch him and missed.

"It's okay, I'm here," Madoc whispered to her. He gingerly put his arms around her, holding her for a moment as much to comfort himself as her. He could feel the broken bones grating inside her body ... and then he remembered the cat and the water bottle.

The crystal flask on its thong was still slung across his shoulder. He quickly pulled the cork and splashed some of the precious fluid over her body. Then he held her head and poured the remainder into her mouth. She swallowed once, coughed and lay still.

Sprawled across the rocks, Derg's thrashing limbs finally settled into their human form. Then a thousand years of ageing caught up with the creature that had been the master shapechanger, turning skin and bone to ashes. The wind scattered them across the Atlantic.

29

"ARE YOU SURE YOU WON'T COME BACK WITH US?" Robert Stone asked as he walked to the taxi.

Madoc shook his head. "Thanks, but no. I have to get back to my clan."

"Clan?"

Madoc smiled. "The Irish for family. I haven't seen them in a while and I suppose they're missing me."

"I never did fully understand what happened out there," Stone said. "I'm not sure I believe this botched kidnap story either," he added, looking at Madoc.

The boy returned his stare, saying nothing.

Elizabeth Stone gave Madoc a brief hug. "It doesn't matter now. Rachel is safe and you're safe. You'll always be welcome, Madoc. Whenever you decide to visit, just let us know and we'll arrange it."

"Thanks again. Do you mind if I say goodbye to Rachel in private?"

"Not at all." Elizabeth looked at her husband, then nodded towards the taxi. "Let's get in."

Rachel and Madoc walked a short distance away, then stopped and turned to face one another. "How do you feel?" he asked.

"Fine," she said briskly. Then her smile faded and fear darkened her eyes. "Not really, Madoc. I'm ... still scared."

He put his arm around her shoulders. "Don't be. It's over, I mean it."

"It's the full moon in three days, Madoc. What if it happens again? What if the cure didn't work?"

"Then we'll find something else, okay? We'll find a cure that *does* work."

"What are you going to do now?" she asked.

"Go back to my clan ... my new clan."

"The Clan Allta," Rachel said. "They'll need a new leader. Someone to bring them out into the world, but keep them safe."

"It'll be easier now that they can control the were-change."

"You'll come and see me sometime?"

"I will," Madoc promised. He looked at her for a second, then gave her an awkward, self-conscious hug. "I'll miss you, Rachel."

"I know. I'll miss you too."

He stepped back. "You'd better go before I start crying."

Rachel nodded. Her own tears were burning behind her eyes. She kissed him lightly on the cheek, then walked to the taxi and climbed in.

As the taxi pulled away, Rachel rolled down the window. "I'll be back!" she shouted.

She did not hear his heartfelt response. "I hope not," whispered Madoc. "I sincerely hope not."

OTHER BOOKS FROM THE O'BRIEN PRESS

OCTOBER MOON
Michael Scott

When Rachel Stone arrives in Ireland with her parents to their new stud farm in County Kildare, strange things happen. Someone – or something – wants to get rid of them. For Rachel, it is a life or death situation. *A really scary story, with a shocking ending.*

£3.99 pb

GEMINI GAME
Michael Scott

Twins Liz and BJ create their own virtual reality game, 'Night's Castle', but when players fall into a strange coma, the twins are in deep trouble. They journey into the VR world, to find that the creatures they have invented have now turned against them.

£3.99 pb

HOUSE OF THE DEAD
Michael Scott

Patrick and Claire have unwittingly unleashed the powers of the ancient burial chamber at Newgrange. What chance have two teenagers against the Great Evil, feared for many centuries?

£3.99 pb

MOONLIGHT
Michael Carroll

A prehistoric, headless horse is found in a glacier. Then Cathy Donnelly gets a holiday job on a stud farm looking after a strange-looking colt, Moonlight. When Moonlight escapes, Cathy goes with him, and the two become enmeshed in a wild chase across country in an attempt to defeat the crazy scientist, Dr Feyermann.

£3.99 pb

THE HUNTER'S MOON
Orla Melling

Adventure, mystery, and the sorcery and magic of the Other World combine when Findabhair disappears and her cousin Gwen sets out to find her.

£3.99 pb

THE DRUID'S TUNE
Orla Melling

Caught up in the enchantments of a modern-day druid, Rosemary and Jimmy are hurled into the ancient past. They have the adventure of their lives in the unusual company of Cuchulainn and Queen Maeve.

£4.50 pb

CELTIC MAGIC TALES
Liam Mac Uistin

Four magical legends from Ireland's Celtic past: the Tuatha de Danann and their king's love-quest; a fantastic and humorous tale of Cuchulainn; the story of Deirdre and the Sons of Usnach; the heroic tale of the Sons of Tuireann.

£3.99 pb

AMELIA
Siobhán Parkinson

The year is 1914 and there are rumours of war in the air. But all that matters to Amelia is what she will wear to her thirteenth birthday party. But when disaster strikes her family, Amelia must hold them together.

£3.99 pb

STAR DANCER
Morgan Llywelyn

When Ger breaks into the RDS horse show, he sees a new world, and he desperately wants to be part of it. Suzanne, riding her horse Star Dancer, has a target too: she wants to train for the Olympics. Their dreams overlap, with interesting results.

£3.99 pb

STRONGBOW
Morgan Llywelyn

The dramatic story of the arrival in Ireland of the Normans, and of Strongbow's life with his new wife, the young Irish princess Aoife. Vivid and exciting history with a strong story.

£3.99 pb

BRIAN BORU
Morgan Llywelyn

The most famous of Ireland's heroes – this is his life story from childhood to the Battle of Clontarf.

£3.95pb

UNDER THE HAWTHORN TREE
Marita Conlon-McKenna

The heartfelt, dramatic account of the children of the Great Irish Famine – Eily, Michael and Peggy – who make a long journey on their own to find the great-aunts they have heard about in their mother's stories.

£3.95 pb

WILDFLOWER GIRL
Marita Conlon-McKenna

Peggy, now thirteen, sets out for America to find a new life. She goes into service in a large Boston house, and must find her own feet in the difficult world of the emigrant.

£4.50 pb

THE BLUE HORSE
Marita Conlon-McKenna

When Katie's family's home burns down they are left destitute. Now she must find a way to hold the family together and must try to fit into a completely new life. But will she be accepted?

£3.99 pb

HORSE THIEF
Hugh Galt

Rory's old horse is stolen, and to prevent it happening again he runs away with her in the night. But they soon come across another horse hidden in the depths of the country. Then begins the wildest chase, in an attempt to save both horses.

£3.99 pb

THE LOST ISLAND
Eilís Dillon

Is the lost island real or fantasy? And who is brave enough to try to find it and gain the treasure? Michael and Joe set off on their boat to reveal the secret of the island.

£3.95 pb

THE CRUISE OF THE SANTA MARIA
Eilís Dillon

John sets sail in a splendid Galway hooker, ending up on a deserted island, empty except for one unusual inhabitant. Here begins a strange adventure, full of exciting, tense moments.

£4.50 pb

The O'Brien Press, 20 Victoria Road, Dublin 6, Ireland
Tel: (01) 923333 Fax: (01) 922777

Add to total, 15% for postage, 25% for airmail

I enclose cheque/postal order for £......
Please charge my credit card ☐ ACCESS ☐ MASTERCARD ☐ VISA

Card:

Expiry:

Name...
Address..
....